BEYOND GUILT

David Berardelli

BEYOND GUILT

GRAVESTONE PRESS

Gravestone Press
is an imprint of
Fiction4All
www.fiction4all.com

This Edition
Published 2022

Cover Art: Linda York

PART ONE – BRAD

Chapter 1

The man was tall and slender, dressed in dark clothing and carrying an odd-shaped black satchel in the crook of his arm, and his eyes stayed fixed on my headlights as my BMW slammed into him.

Everything from that point slowed down and turned fuzzy and out of focus, like a dream sequence in a weird movie. The streetlamps and traffic lights straight ahead faded, blending into a gooey mess of shapeless colors, and the passing traffic disappeared. Everything had turned into a vast dark stillness.

A feeling of iciness enveloped me as if someone had draped a wet towel across my shoulders. The only thing that existed right then was the horrible thud the man's body had made when my car plowed into him. The disgusting sound resonated through me, filling my being. Mixed with the frantic beating of my heart, the overall effect was deafening. My first instinct was to cover my ears, but I needed to keep a tight grip on the wheel. Even so, the nauseating sound continued resonating, growing louder, like some wild African tribal beat.

I suddenly realized that the sound would intensify if I covered my ears. Doing that might hold it all in. But I had to do *some*thing to take my mind off it.

I massaged my temples. Then I rubbed my eyes. Only then did I discover that my hands were no longer gripping the steering wheel. I'd apparently stopped driving without even being aware of it.

The BMW was no longer moving. The traffic lights remained where they'd been moments ago, suggesting that I hadn't gone very far since the accident. I was sitting behind the wheel, staring at the intersection a hundred or so yards straight ahead, where the lights had just turned red. There was no traffic waiting there.

I wondered where everyone had gone.

Had the rest of the world disappeared? Or had I somehow escaped this horror? Had I departed this life altogether? Had the mind-blowing act of slamming into a person on the highway forced me to veer off the road and mash my vehicle into the nearest building, killing me as well?

Or had my existence simply changed, blending into the strange foggy blackness that had taken hold of me?

I continued staring at the lights. They'd already turned green. A few cars came my way, creeping through the intersection. They were moving much slower than moments ago, when I'd made my hasty departure from cold reality. Just before they passed, they all merged into a single lane.

Were they being directed to merge? Or were they simply trying to avoid something lying in the road behind me?

I forced myself to believe that the traffic didn't matter. Nothing mattered because I was no longer a part of the picture. I had no intention of grabbing the wheel and continuing my journey home. In fact, I had no intention of doing anything. That was a no-brainer, since I suddenly realized I was unable to move.

I *had* to move, didn't I? I couldn't just sit here for the rest of my life. I was alive, wasn't I? Being alive was part of life, wasn't it? People who no longer moved were usually dead or lying in a coma in a hospital bed.

Since I wasn't in a coma, I decided that I should continue acting the part of a living, breathing human being.

I decided to explore my surroundings.

I was surprised to discover that I was no longer on the highway. At some point during the last few agonizing moments, I'd veered off the road and pulled into a strip mall—although I had no recollection of doing so. I had no recollection of doing anything once I'd slammed into the guy who'd stepped out in front of me.

Had that actually happened? Or had I imagined it?

The mind does strange things when you're exhausted or stressed. I'd been pushing myself the last few weeks. The office had literally gone crazy since the new merger had graduated from whispered rumors to direct action. Everyone was nervous, suspicious of the new faces wandering about. Conference calls and meetings had taken up most of my afternoons, and I hadn't had time to do anything but drive to work, preside over the meetings, argue about business strategies with the new faces, drive home, fix dinner and sack out. Half the time, I'd collapsed in the living room recliner the instant I got home. The other times, I'd nodded off even before I was able to finish my meal. I'd been running on all eight cylinders for much too long and needed a rest. When you're in such a vulnerable state, all sorts of weird, unexplained things can happen.

I had to consider that my imagination had been playing tricks on me. I remembered the times during the last few days when I'd left the house without my keys or cell phone. Yesterday afternoon, I poured a cup of coffee, took a call on my cell and left the cafeteria without taking the coffee with me. Two days ago, I pulled out the makings of a sandwich from the fridge, got a call, went to my den to look for some papers and left the bread, turkey, cheese, pickles, and the mayo jar on the counter until the next morning.

My brain had been on overload for too long and definitely needed a recharge.

But would it make me imagine that I'd run over someone? Would it go to such an extent to create such a horrible vision?

Maybe I *had* imagined it. At least, I *hoped* I had...

How could I find out for sure? How could I know? What would it take to convince me that my overworked brain had simply provided me with a hallucination to force me to take it easy?

Just turn around and see for yourself.

That sounded simple enough, didn't it?

If I saw nothing, I'd know right then that I needed a rest. This time, I'd actually pay attention to the signs and do what was necessary. I'd call in early the next morning and tell Gloria I wasn't feeling well and needed some time off. If a few days weren't enough, I'd call in again and tell her I was going to take off the following week. I had vacation time coming; they could handle things without me. If not, I'd obviously hired the wrong people.

All I had to do to fix this was turn around and see for myself that there was no body, that my exhausted brain had imagined the whole thing. I hadn't run over anyone. I was extremely tired and might even have dozed off or just zoned out for a moment or two. I might have hit a stray dog, for all I knew—or someone's discarded Arby's bag. A number of things might have happened, things that weren't so serious or traumatic…

But that didn't mean I *hadn't* run over someone, did it?

No. That terrible possibility clung stubbornly to my mind.

I continued sitting behind the wheel, my pulse hammering as I gathered the courage to turn around. Could I do this? Did I have the balls necessary to face my fear? What if I *had* run someone over? Could I deal with it? Could I live with the knowledge that I'd actually killed another human being?

9

It doesn't matter. You have to find out. It's the only way you'll be able to get through this moment.

Because, no matter what happened or didn't happen, you can't just sit here like this!

After about a minute, I found the courage inside me and turned around.

My heart practically leaped out of my chest.

About a hundred feet behind me, a dark, motionless figure lay just off the curb. His crumpled satchel sat in the middle of the road, about twenty feet from the figure's outstretched hand. A few yards from where the figure lay, two police cruisers, lights flashing, blocked the lane. One cop directed the traffic in the other lane, merging both lanes into one so as not to disturb the scene.

The other cop was talking to the radio attached to his left shoulder as he cautiously approached my car.

Chapter 2

I turned to face the front, closed my eyes and willed myself to be somewhere else. This wasn't happening; it just *couldn't* be. I hadn't done this. I refused to believe that I'd just mowed down another human being as if...as if—

As if he wasn't there in the first place?

Yes. That was it. He *wasn't* there. I was driving down the road, minding my own business...and there he was. He'd just *appeared*—had simply *materialized* in front of my car. It was as if he'd been snatched from some other universe and placed right there in front of me, just one moment before I—

The harsh rap on my window sounded similar to the thump the body had made, and I jumped.

Pull yourself together. You can do this. There's a cop out there and he's trying to get your attention. You can't come apart at the seams now, can you?

I could hold myself together; I'd done it countless times before, hadn't I? I was a grown man. I'd been married and divorced twice. Both women had soaked me, but I'd survived. I'd been running Ellis & Associates the last nine years and had kept it going in spite of the twists and turns the economy had taken. The Dow had dipped, dropped and stumbled more than a dozen times during those years, but we'd survived. I even managed to keep the company going without laying off people or lowering salaries. My employees respected me and trusted me. Many of them even liked me.

I could definitely handle something like this.

Can you? I asked myself. *This isn't about the economy, and it sure as hell isn't about two women who divorced you because you spent more time at the office than you did with them. This is the real thing. This is vehicular manslaughter, and you'd better start taking it seriously…*

Another rap.

"Sir? Please roll down your window…"

Reality had intervened again. *Listen to it,* my inner voice persisted. *If you don't, you'll be truly sorry.*

Pull yourself together. Think. Focus.

I took a couple of deep breaths. *There. So far, so good…* I rubbed my eyes, tapped my cheeks and tried to focus. *I'm Brad Ellis*, I reminded myself. *I'm sitting here behind the wheel of my BMW and I'm in one piece.* To make sure I was right, I rubbed my palms together. *Yep. One piece. And my pants are still dry.*

Now…focus on what's next…

The window. He wanted me to lower the window. It couldn't be *that* difficult, could it? A man boasting as many accomplishments as I just did should surely be able to perform such an incredibly simple task.

For some reason, I found pressing the damned button just as complicated as deciding which wire to cut on a bomb. The button was right there on the door rest, just as visible and as accessible as ever. It

12

was there when I bought the car and had been there ever since. I'd never had trouble with it before...

Even so, I had trouble reaching it. My arm suddenly weighed a ton, and my hand shook too much. To make things even worse, I kept pulling away from it. Did I *want* to keep from lowering it? Was this a subconscious attempt to keep the remnants of my world from escaping? Or was this my feeble way to keep out the chilling reality of what I'd just done?

Whatever it was, I knew I couldn't hold it off for long. It would infuriate the cop and make the situation worse. But I just couldn't help it.

Another rap.

"Sir?" He sounded impatient.

You can do this, dammit!

I know I can...

What are you waiting for, then?

Gritting my teeth, I forced my arm closer to the door rest. After some furious groping, I pressed the button. The window slid quietly down, and a wash of ice flowed in, chilling me to the bone.

Ice? In Florida? I really *was* losing it...

"Sir? You all right?" The cop sounded genuinely concerned.

"I'm really sorry..." I couldn't think of anything else to say right then. I wanted to tell him why I couldn't open the window at first but guessed by his expression that he'd probably already figured it out. "I'm kind of...well, messed up right now... I couldn't manage...the window button...I just...I couldn't *find* the damned thing!"

13

"Sir, would you please step out of your vehicle?"

"P-Pardon me?"

"Please step out, sir. I need to ask you a few questions."

Once again, my body had betrayed me. I knew where the door latch was, but couldn't grab it. I wanted to switch on the interior light to see it better but didn't want the cop to think I was up to something. I'd never been in this situation before but had seen enough cop shows to know that they had to be suspicious of every move a suspect made during a traffic stop. For all he knew, I could have guns or drugs in the car. After all, I'd just slammed into someone and possibly even killed him. This man had to be especially cautious.

But after a minute or so, he seemed to sense my dilemma and reached inside to pull open the door himself.

"Thank you."

He nodded but said nothing. He had small light-blue or gray eyes. In the haze of the streetlamp, I couldn't quite tell what color they were. They'd looked cold at first, but I could actually see a softness emanating from them.

I started to slide out and quickly got hung up on my seat belt. *Dammit. This man is really gonna think I'm drunk!*

"My seat belt. I guess I forgot all about it..." It was all I could think of that made any sense.

"Go 'head and release it," he said.

To my utter astonishment, I managed to do it without strangling myself.

"Please step out, sir…"

I nearly collapsed when the hard pavement tapped the bottoms of my shoes. He helped me by grabbing my arm, and I straightened and leaned against the side of the BMW for support. I wanted to give him an explanation for my clumsiness but realized it might make my situation even worse, if that was at all possible. After a few tense moments, I discovered that I could stand on my own. I forced myself from turning to my left, where my victim lay on the highway. The first time I'd seen him, it nearly destroyed me. I couldn't possibly manage it again right now.

"Sir?"

The officer was speaking to me.

"Yes?"

"Are you all right?"

That was the most ridiculous thing anyone had ever asked me. I wanted to tell him how I felt, but something inside me told me to choose my next words wisely. With this in mind, I gave him a subtle version of what was going on in my head at that moment. "No. I'm not. I just hit someone. I'm *not* all right. As a matter of fact, I don't think I'll ever be all right again…"

As he watched me, I could see his eyes softening again. He looked down at his pad and stared at it. I could tell he was trying to give me as much time as he could under the circumstances. He obviously saw something on my face he seemed to

15

understand—something he might have seen before. He knew right off that this was definitely something that needed to be handled delicately. However, he had a job to do. I knew that as well as he did.

"Sir, do you need to be taken to the hospital?"

"I honestly don't know. I don't think I'm hurt…"

He held up his index finger about a foot in front of my face. "Can you see this?"

I nodded.

"Keep your eyes on my finger, but don't move your head."

He moved it back and forth across my line of vision, very slowly. Afterward, he lowered his arm. I knew what he was doing. "Have you been drinking, sir?"

"No…"

"You've had nothing at all to drink?"

"I don't drink and drive. I stopped doing that in college when I developed a brain cell or two."

He seemed satisfied with my answer and wrote something down in his notebook. "I need to see your license, registration, and proof of insurance."

I reached for my back pocket. As soon as I did, I realized that I'd forgotten which pocket I kept my wallet in. This made my urge to panic even more immediate. I'd been carrying my wallet in the same pocket since I was old enough to drive. That was more than twenty years ago. I shouldn't have any trouble at all finding it right now.

Hell, you couldn't even lower the window two minutes ago!

This was indeed a critical situation, and if I wasn't careful, I'd make a horrible mess of it. If I bungled anything else, this man would certainly force me to take a sobriety test. But I had no choice. Once again, I forced myself to do whatever it took to keep the panic away.

Think, Ellis. One thing at a time.

Then, finally, it came to me. I carried my wallet in the rear pocket on my right side, where I'd been carrying it since I first got my learner's permit.

I pulled it out and fumbled for the right cards, but my hands just wouldn't cooperate, and I dropped the damned thing. It landed with a *splat*! on the pavement between my feet. I stood there like an idiot, staring down at it as if I had no idea what I'd just done or what I should do next.

"I'm really sorry," I said. I wanted to tell him that this was the first time I'd ever been involved in something like this. I decided against it. It would have come out wrong no matter how I said it and would have made me sound like a demented idiot. Or worse—a drunken, demented idiot.

"It's all right." He bent to snatch it up and handed it back to me. This time I took special care opening it. I successfully pulled out my driver's license and registration without dropping them again. Then I handed them over. As he studied them, I found my insurance card and gave it to him as well.

"One moment, please..." He turned and went back to his cruiser.

I stood there stiffly, forcing myself not to gawk at the scene. Several other vehicles had shown up. I still hadn't turned in that direction, but I could hear the engines idling and several different voices barking orders and instructions. The medical unit was probably there, and perhaps another police cruiser. I turned to face the BMW, rested my elbows on its flawless finish and tried very hard to keep myself from coming apart. I closed my eyes again and struggled to convince myself that this was not actually happening. I was not really here; I'd imagined all this. I visualized my Winter Park condo and even saw myself in the shower, scrubbing down after another torturous day at the office. I could even see the drink I'd fixed when I came home—a double Scotch and soda. It was waiting for me on the kitchen counter as soon as I stepped out of the shower, toweled myself dry and—

"Mr. Ellis?"

The strangely familiar voice behind me jarred me forcibly out of my daydream.

Pull yourself together!

Taking a deep breath, I straightened and turned around. I was about to ask the cop how he knew my name. He was standing a few feet away, holding out my cards. I stared at them, then at him, and after a few awkward moments realized that he knew my name because he'd been checking my cards. Once that mystery was solved, I began to wonder what I was supposed to do. He pushed them closer, and the scrap of reason still clinging to my brain suggested I

18

take them. They were mine, weren't they? He was handing them to me because he obviously didn't need them anymore.

It's really a no-brainer. You majored in math and business management, and even made fairly good grades in Algebra and Trigonometry. You surely can figure out something this simple.

I took them and put them in my shirt pocket rather than try slipping them back in my wallet. I had to do whatever was necessary to keep from dropping things again.

"We'll need to ask you a few questions, Mr. Ellis. Would you mind taking a trip to the Police Station?"

I wanted to ask him if I was under arrest. He hadn't asked me to turn around, so I figured he wasn't about to cuff me.

"We have coffee at the Station," he said. "If you need medical assistance—"

"Can you drive me?" I asked. "I'm too...too shaken up—"

"I understand. If you need someone to park and secure your car, we can do that."

"I'd appreciate it. The keys are in the ignition."

"Can you make it to the cruiser? Or do you need a hand?"

"I think I can make it, thanks."

Chapter 3

Strange things happened to me during the short ride to the Police Station in downtown Orlando.

The moment the police cruiser began moving, my body grew warm and numb, and I no longer felt the seat I was sitting on. When I closed my eyes, I could no longer hear the steady hum of the engine. I actually felt myself rising, until I was suspended in the air. This startled me, and when I opened my eyes, it took several frustrating moments to realize what was actually happening.

I'd apparently been struggling to transport myself somewhere else while trying to ignore the reality of what had happened. When I finally acknowledged the fact that I wasn't able to transport myself anywhere, I began thinking of my childhood, when life was much simpler. I remembered the times my older brother and I got into mischief, how we'd both panicked when we realized what would happen if we were ever caught red-handed. Back then, our "mischief" had always been minor. The "crimes" usually amounted to a cracked windowpane, a spilled paint can, a bb dent or two in the furniture or on Dad's car, or an occasional scraped knee or elbow. As a kid, life was seldom frightening; with both parents running the household, our sense of security kept the fears and shortcomings of reality at arm's length. As a kid, one never thought of running someone over, killing someone, or being carted off to the Police Station.

And death was something a child thought of only when a friend, relative or beloved pet died.

Before I realized it, the police car had stopped, wrenching me out of my comfortable state of nostalgia. The door opened and reality gushed in, bringing with it exhaust fumes and other unpleasant smells of the city. A broad-shouldered figure in blue stood just a few feet away from the open door, waiting for me to get out. The cloud in my head dissipated and I finally accepted what was going on.

I got out, gazed at the well-lit building straight ahead and vaguely remembered that we'd reached the parking lot of the Police Station. That was fairly clear, but as soon as we started walking, my nightmare returned, my surroundings faded instantly and blurred all over again. I was vaguely aware that I was walking with someone, and that we were approaching a building…but not much else. Everything had slowed down again and turned fuzzy. We were halfway down the brightly lit hall before the indistinct shapes passing us cleared, turning into the images of figures in blue as well as others of both sexes dressed in suits or other civilian attire. Some glanced at us as we passed, but mostly everyone stared straight ahead, indicating a sense of isolation—of being content in their own little world.

Luckily for me, the place wasn't very crowded at this late hour. I considered it a blessing in disguise; I just couldn't bear people staring at me. I was fully aware that I wasn't capable of completely holding in the nightmare; I didn't want anyone glimpsing even a small portion of it showing on my face.

I'd glanced at a wall clock as we went down the hall but couldn't make out the time. The glare from the ceiling fluorescents had turned the center of the clock face into a jagged white starburst. It had to be close to midnight. I'd left the office at ten that night and had been halfway home when the accident happened. Since it usually took me half an hour to get to Winter Park, I figured the nightmare had occurred at approximately 10:15. I didn't know how long I'd sat in the BMW before the cop knocked on my window. Since something like this would have been called in fairly quickly, it might have been ten, maybe fifteen minutes, tops, before the cop approached my vehicle. It took another couple of minutes to roll down my window and possibly five more before I was asked to get out of the car. This brought it to around 10:30 or 10:40…

I tried calculating how long it had taken us to get from Colonial Drive to the Police Station. With traffic, it took close to half an hour. At this time of night? No more than fifteen or twenty minutes. On weekends, with the Magic games, it took much longer—but that was only during basketball season.

Was it basketball season? I couldn't remember. I couldn't even remember what day of the week it was. I vaguely recalled it being early September, but nothing else seemed to be clicking now.

Maybe it was closer to eleven than midnight. Maybe—

Did it really make *any* difference what time of day or night this happened? Or even what day? Or if it was or wasn't basketball season? I'd *run over someone*, for God's sake. Did it matter what *time*—or *day*—or *season*—the accident took place?

I forced myself to go back and pick up the details that *did* matter—things that had happened in my life before everything suddenly took a nosedive. Vera had called earlier—around six, as I recalled. She'd called to ask if I was going to come over and see her before I went home. I had to beg off because I had some work to catch up on. I'd told her I was exhausted and would be lousy company. We'd only recently begun seeing one another, so I didn't really expect her to go along with that. But she did and said we could try and hook up tomorrow at lunch if she could get away from the hair salon. I'd been much too tired and distracted to argue.

While I found myself on this senseless trip back in time, I went back maybe an hour or so before the accident and began changing the sequence of things to alter the end result—how I'd left the office in such a damned hurry, creeping through that yellow light on Robinson instead of stopping early, letting it turn red, then waiting that extra minute or two before it turned green again...

If only I'd dropped my keys before leaving my office...or answered that last call as I was putting on my jacket instead of letting it go to voicemail...

If only I'd stopped at that damned yellow light...

23

If I'd done anything differently, it would have changed the flow of events. In fact, it would have changed everything just by adjusting the time frame—tweaking where I was and when I was, just a second or so sooner or later. It wouldn't have taken much at all to change the outcome. One slight nudge in either direction would have put me in a different spot entirely, and I wouldn't have been there at that precise moment to slam into that poor man.

This nightmare wouldn't have happened at all if I'd gone to see Vera instead of heading straight home. I wouldn't have had to drop my keys in my office or stop at the yellow light on Robinson. If I'd gone to see her, I wouldn't have been on Colonial Drive at all, and wouldn't have run into the man.

Oh, to be home, or with Vera in her apartment...

It sounded so inconceivable now...so unattainable...

I was looking at my life now as if returning to it had somehow reached the same unattainable level as climbing Mount Everest.

Would my life ever be the same again? Would I ever be able to go back to it?

I was led into one of their small interview rooms and offered one of four chairs positioned beneath a metal table. They said they'd get back with me in a few minutes, then closed the door and left me by myself.

I found the thin-cushioned chair strangely comfortable. For some reason I could not quite understand, it felt just as cushy as the ergonomically correct chair in my office, which went for more than two grand. It apparently had something to do with my present state of shock. I sat forward, my elbows on the table, my hands covering my face as I listened to the soft, steady hum of the fluorescents directly above my head. I'd zoned out again and, as before, wished myself in a different place.

Before long, reality came thundering back, reminding me why I was sitting all alone in an interview room at the Police Station.

I'd slammed into someone with my car. It was that simple.

My God... Had I really done such a horrible, incredibly stupid thing?

Was the man dead? Or was he just injured?

Had I ended his life?

I buried my face in my hands and fought down the urge to let the panic rush in. I wanted to scream, to slam my head onto the hard surface of the table. I wanted to go back twenty-four hours...or twelve...or just a couple—whatever it took to get me back to where I'd been moments before I'd hit the poor guy.

If only I'd gone to see Vera...

If only I hadn't stayed that extra hour...

"*Shit!*" The word exploded hotly from my throat. It seemed to be coming from someone else— someone with no inhibitions and nothing to lose. Someone who needed to say what was in his heart and didn't care much for the consequences. "*Shit! Shit! Shit!*"

Then I heard the door behind me clicking open.

Chapter 4

Two men blocked the doorway.

One was the cop who'd brought me, the other a short, broad man in a tan suit and olive-green tie. He had a salt-and-pepper brush cut, heavy black brows, deep-set green eyes, and was probably around fifty. Both men looked worried as they watched me. They seemed reluctant to enter the room. I assumed they'd been watching me through the glass wall and were waiting for my rant to end. I just sighed and slumped in my chair. The rant, brief as it was, had taken a toll on me, making me even more exhausted and stressed.

I saw no reason to make this horrible situation worse. I straightened in my seat as they closed the door behind them and approached the table. They pulled out the two chairs opposite me and sat. They both looked grim. They were probably wondering if I needed medical help. Or maybe they understood what I was going through. Either way, I was embarrassed for my outburst and realized I needed to show them I didn't normally act this way. I was a corporate executive and knew how to handle all sorts of people on a daily basis. I was known as the guy with good nerves, someone you could trust…and was proud that I'd never lost my cool at any meeting or conference.

But this was something I'd never encountered before. I'd just been involved in a horrible traffic accident and its effects had chilled me to the bone.

Still, I knew it wouldn't be very bright to display any emotion that might make them consider me unstable.

"Are you all right, Mr. Ellis?" the cop asked. He'd placed a brown folder on the table in front of him but hadn't opened it. His companion hadn't taken his eyes off me since they'd come into the room.

They were both obviously waiting for me to display behavior that might explain a possible mental imbalance. They needed something that would get them to close the books on this so they didn't have to waste too many man-hours investigating it.

"As I told you before," I told the cop, "I don't think I'll ever be all right again."

He nodded. I saw the same sympathy in his light-gray eyes as I did before. His black nametag said *SILVER*. It was the first time I noticed it. For one crazy moment I wondered if his first name was John, and if anyone called him Long John. I knew better than say that aloud. It might prompt them to send me to their department shrink. It irritated me to know that my brain was suddenly operating as it had when I was a silly juvenile.

Perhaps the act of running over a man had done something serious to my head.

"We understand," he said.

The man beside him nodded. "I'm Detective Adam Rossberg," he said flatly. "Sorry to meet under these circumstances."

I acknowledged him with a nod and stared at my hands. The words came out of my throat even before I thought they would. "The man I…the guy I ran into… Is he…is he…dead?"

They both nodded grimly.

Slivers of ice made my flesh tingle, and I shivered.

"We need to know what happened," Silver said.

I didn't reply.

"Mr. Ellis?"

"I thought you knew. I ran into the guy on Colonial."

"We understand," Rossberg said. "What we need to know is *how* it happened."

I stared at my clenched fists as if the answer lay trapped within them. Then I opened my hands and saw nothing in them. When I realized just how foolish I was being, that the answer lay somewhere amidst the cluttered mess that had once been my brain, I closed my eyes and tried to remember. I quickly discovered that there wasn't much to it. I'd slammed into someone with my car—what else could I add to that?

"It…just happened." I noticed only then that my voice sounded pitiful and weak.

The two of them waited for me to go into detail. Finally Officer Silver said, "Are you saying—"

"I'm saying it just *happened*. Like that." I tried clicking my fingers but managed to make a shambles of that, as well. Since my nerves were obviously shot, I had to do it twice. "I was driving down the road. All of a sudden, the man was just standing there."

"Just *standing* there?" Rossberg asked.

"He just *appeared*. One moment, the stretch all the way to the light was clear. The very next, the guy was standing right there, watching me.

"You didn't see where he came from?" Silver asked.

I thought for a moment. "There was a small parking lot on my right, just a few feet from the curb. There was also a parked van." The image flashed before me then blurred into darkness with the rest of the memories. "He might have been behind it, out of my line of vision, making his way toward the highway as I approached."

"And you couldn't swerve out of the way?"

I felt my hands becoming fists again. I let them stay that way. "I couldn't do *anything*. He was *right there*."

They both stared at me, then at each other.

After some thought, Silver asked, "And he made no effort to move out of the way?"

It took every bit of control I had left to get the words out of my throat. When they came out, they emerged sluggishly—as if they'd been warm and perfectly content in the safety of my voice box and hadn't wanted to leave their happy home. "He didn't move. He was standing right there, as motionless as a statue, watching me as I hit him. It was almost like…like he was in some sort of trance."

Once again the two of them remained silent, but I could see some doubt in their faces as they watched me.

"A trance?" Silver asked. "Are you saying—"

"I just said he was watching me hit him. He didn't even flinch."

Rossberg nodded.

I was tempted to ask why he was nodding, but part of me didn't want to know. The other part decided he was nodding because they'd obviously found out something that went along with my story. I knew better than ask. If it was important, they'd tell me. If not, I didn't have to know. I had entirely too much clouding my mind already.

"I suppose that would explain what we found out," Silver said.

"What would?" Maybe I actually did want to find out what really happened.

"The lab reports," Rossberg said. "When he was brought in, his blood was tested. The alcohol level was found to be .21 percent."

"My God. Are you sure?"

He nodded.

"That's nearly—"

"Three times the legal limit, had he been driving," Silver said. "But even so, he shouldn't have been trying to cross a busy highway in that condition."

"They also found a significant amount of cocaine in his system," Rossberg added.

I slumped in my chair.

"Are you all right?" Silver asked.

I just shook my head.

"You should be relieved," Rossberg said.

I couldn't believe he'd said that. It made the hair on the back of my neck bristle. The man was drunk and had coke in his system. Because of this, it was perfectly all right for him to be run over and killed?

"Why in heaven's name should I be relieved?"

Rossberg knew right then that he'd said something inappropriate. He was silent for a moment before he spoke again. "I only meant that you weren't at fault. The man was highly intoxicated and had ingested a large amount of cocaine. He shouldn't have been out by himself, and he certainly shouldn't have been standing in the middle of one of the busiest stretches of highway in Orlando at night. He stepped into oncoming traffic. You were blameless in this."

Blameless. It made it sound almost as if I'd been *justified* in killing the man. Instead of letting my rage come right out, I took a breath and hoped it would calm me a little. It didn't, but I had to get it out anyway. "I *killed* a man. I don't *feel* blameless. In fact, I feel anything *but* blameless. If you want to know how I really feel, I'll put it this way—I'm totally surprised that I haven't already heaved my guts."

They just looked at me.

I sat forward and rubbed my temples. My head was pounding. I felt nauseous and even more depressed than I was when they'd first brought me in. Learning that the man I'd killed had done coke and was staggering around drunk failed to soften any of this. I'd been drunk several times in my life, too, and had done coke a few times as well. I never got behind the wheel of a car in such a condition, nor did I ever try to cross a busy highway while heavily intoxicated or high…

Even so, I didn't know the circumstances leading up to this. For all I knew, the man might not have even known what he was doing or where he was at the time.

The fact remained: I'd killed him, and nothing would ever be right again.

"Mr. Ellis?" Rossberg sounded concerned.

"Yes?"

"Would you like to go home now?"

"Now?"

"Yes…"

"You don't need me here anymore?"

"There'll be some papers you'll have to sign, of course. A few waivers, and a personal eyewitness statement, both signed and notarized. You weren't drinking or speeding. You were unable to avoid the man, who obviously had no idea where he was or what he was doing. This was merely an unfortunate accident."

"What about a possible lawsuit?"

Rossberg shrugged. "That'll be handled by our legal department. If there is one brought in, you'll be notified as soon as possible. But given the circumstances, I don't see the family pursuing this. They'll be given a detailed account of the accident.

If they wish to proceed with damages, as I just said, you'll be notified."

"I don't see it happening," Silver said. "So don't worry about it unless it comes up."

Rossberg nodded. "As far as we're concerned, you're free to go."

"What about him?" I asked.

"Who do you mean?" Rossberg asked.

I sighed and told myself to stay calm. I was in a Police Station, after all. I may have just skated through a vehicular homicide but losing my cool and throwing a tantrum certainly wouldn't slip by unnoticed. "The man I ran over. What about him?"

They both sat in silence and looked confused. They obviously had no idea what I was talking about.

"I'm talking about his relatives, his friends…"

"They'll be notified," Silver said. "His next of kin has already been called. Standard procedure, of course."

For some reason, none of that seemed to matter. The only thing I couldn't get over was that I'd killed someone and was able to leave the Police Station as if nothing happened. "What was his name?"

"Pardon?"

"The man's name. What was it?"

The men exchanged awkward glances.

Silver said, "Sir, we really don't think—"

"What was his name?" It was suddenly vitally important that I learned the man's name. I had to know something about him, even if it was just his name.

Silver opened the folder. "The man's name was Morrison. Daniel Glen Morrison." He closed the folder.

"What else?" Now that I'd learned his name, I found that I wanted to know more.

"Pardon?"

"I'd like to know a little about the man I just murdered."

"Why?" Rossberg appeared nauseated.

I couldn't really blame them for not understanding me. They dealt with death all the time and had been trained to stick with procedure. It probably bothered them early on in their careers, but I imagined that after a few dozen of these cases, it gradually became nothing more than getting the right forms filled out and sent to the correct department before moving on.

"The man was alive up until the moment I first saw him. He had a life. A job. A home. He was probably married. He might have had kids."

Rossberg remained scowling. "Sir, this has nothing to do with what happened…"

"It has everything to do with *me*!"

"Why?" Silver asked.

"I'm the one who took it all away from him!" The words scraped painfully out of my throat like splinters of glass.

Silence.

Silver finally pulled his chair back and stood. "Mr. Ellis, we really think you need to get home.

You're exhausted, overwrought, and you'll feel much better once you're home and—"

"I'd feel much better if I knew just a little about the man I just snuffed out, thanks very much."

"We don't usually like to—"

"It'll be in the *Sentinel*, won't it? On the news? Cable One? MSNBC might even snatch it up if they've got a slow week. I'll probably even see something about it on Facebook, and if the man knew a bunch of people or had friends, we'll all be seeing a slew of irritating tweets. And don't forget You Tube. And if anyone was out there tonight with a cell phone that takes clear pictures—"

"Very well." Silver sat back down and opened the folder again. "Mr. Morrison was thirty. He lived in an apartment on Rio Grande. He had a girlfriend, but no kids. His parents live in Tampa."

"What did he do for a living?"

Rossberg was beginning to look worried. "Mr. Ellis...*please* let one of our officers drive you back to your car."

I could tell neither wanted to tell me anything else. It made me wonder if they were hiding something, or if they just wanted to end their shift. Either way, they'd both given me clear indication that they were done here.

They both stood. As they turned, I said, "Just tell me one other thing. Please?"

They glanced at one another. Then they both slowly turned to face me.

"That satchel the man was carrying..."

"What about it?" from Rossberg.

"What…was in it?"

Silence.

"Please tell me, and I promise I won't bother you again."

Rossberg sighed. "Why do you wanna know?"

"The way he was clutching it… He was gripping it close to his chest when I hit him. It was obviously valuable to him. When I saw it lying in the middle of the road, his arm was outstretched in its direction. It was almost like…like he was reaching for it, even though he could no longer move…" I took a breath. An avalanche of ice slid down my back, and I suddenly felt as if I could no longer breathe.

Silver's face turned grim. "Mr. Morrison was a musician. He played in a small jazz group that performed in clubs on the Trail, off Colonial, and at Disney Village."

A musician. Somehow, this made things even worse. I'd murdered a musician, for God's sake. A musician, no less. Someone who created music. Someone who made people happy and sad and romantic and many other things, by producing beautiful melodies.

I'd always loved music. I loved classical, popular, jazz, and even country & western. My father had been interested in jazz for most of his life. I still had his collection of jazz albums he'd left me, and played them on his old stereo whenever I had an hour or so of free time.

"The satchel." I swallowed a lump in my throat. "What was in the satchel?"

"A trumpet." Rossberg frowned. "Mr. Morrison played the trumpet."

Silver opened the door. Rossberg left the room. Silver waited for me to stand up and follow them out.

It seemed to take forever, but I pushed myself out of the chair and shuffled out of the room on legs that felt like lead.

Chapter 5

A different cop drove me to the strip mall on Colonial Drive, where they'd parked my BMW after the accident. His nametag said *Reyes,* and he was dark, good-looking, and about thirty years old. As we approached the dreaded area, I lowered my head and forced my eyes shut. Total darkness seemed like a terrific idea.

"You okay, sir?" Officer Reyes asked.

"I just…can't look." I had the feeling that if I looked at the area, I'd see the man still lying there, his arm outstretched, reaching for his satchel. It had happened just a few hours ago, but even though the area had been cleared and Morrison had been taken to the morgue, I'd still see it. There could be blood stains on the pavement, for all I knew. I'd been through more than enough torment in the last couple of hours. I didn't need anything else making things worse.

Reyes made no comment. He obviously understood what I was going through. He pulled off the highway, stopped behind the BMW and waited for me to get out. When I didn't move, he said, "You gonna be all right to drive home, Mr. Ellis?"

"I'm not quite sure. I hope so…"

"Go home. Get some rest. You drink?"

I nodded.

"Fix yourself a drink; you'll feel better. Just don't get back on the road. Go to bed. Try to sleep."

"Thanks." I didn't want to tell him how stupid his advice sounded. I really couldn't expect him to relate to this. It was ridiculous to think that a man who dealt with death and violence on a daily basis could sympathize with someone like me. I ran a company that specialized in distributing security system packages to its subsidiaries, but I certainly didn't deal with death.

I got out, closed the door, and gave him a half-assed wave. Once he saw me take the keys out of my pocket, he pulled away from the curb and drove away. I still couldn't turn to see where the horror had happened.

I soon found that I couldn't approach the car, either. It faced the cell phone store—which was good, since I couldn't see the front of the vehicle. It was also good that the nearest streetlamp was too far away to highlight the storefront glass, which would have enabled me to see the reflection of the front of the car.

I wondered if Daniel Glen Morrison had put a dent in the front panel.

I'd plowed into him at quite a clip. Logic would dictate that he'd leave some sort of lasting impression on the metal.

Would there be blood on the panel? The hint of such a thing made me nauseous again. *Don't think of that. Not now, anyway. Later, after you've had some time to process this, you might be able to consider such grisly details.*

Later? The prospect of such a ludicrous concept was almost amusing. How long could I go before I

40

could face the front of my car without puking or freaking out? Two days? Ten? A month? A year? Would I have to trade the car in just to survive this?

What if there *was* blood spatter on the surface of the front panel? How would I deal with that? Would I just continue to drive it and hope the rain would wash it off? Should I pull into one of those drive-thru carwashes and let the brushes and hoses soap, wash, rinse, and wax everything down to gleaming perfection? Or should I just wait until someone asked me about the blood on the front of my car?

What would I do then? Lie about it? Act clueless? Or simply tell them that I'd run over someone and hadn't the time to have the car washed?

I could call Steve, my mechanic, and ask him to come over to the condo and take the car away for a quick wash-and-wax. I'd offer him a hundred bucks extra for his time. Then I wouldn't have to worry about this anymore.

You've got to stop this nonsense, get in the car, and drive home!

That's what I had to do. I didn't have to look at it right now. And since the damage was out of my range of sight, I could postpone the inevitable—until I got home, anyway.

That seemed a terrific idea. It was the only thing I could think of right now that didn't sound absurd. It was either that, or I could just stand here and continue to vegetate until someone saw me and called the cops to have me hauled away.

You're still alive, so start functioning!

Yes. I still had a brain. I had to start using it again.

I pressed the button on my remote to unlock the doors and did it without dropping it or engaging the horn by mistake. I got behind the wheel, inserted the key, started it up, backed out and flicked on the lights as I pulled out onto the highway.

It was late; traffic was extremely light.

This was a good thing, since I couldn't glance to my left before pulling out. I still couldn't bear to look in that direction.

Luckily for me, no one was coming.

I hoped the trip home would be just as uneventful.

***

I soon discovered that I'd been unduly optimistic.

As I drove down the nearly deserted highway, the BMW began pulling to the right. Since I'd kept the car in tip-top condition from the day I bought it just ten months earlier, I considered it unlikely that something mechanical had gone wrong. However, I just couldn't get the idea out of my head. I even tried a couple of times to correct it by jerking the wheel to the left and nearly sideswiped the Ford pickup passing me at the time.

I had to get control of myself and concentrate on what I was doing. I told myself I was imagining all this. The car was operating exactly as it should. There was no jerking, no pulling, and certainly no veering off to the right.

42

As a precaution, I slowed down to slightly under the posted speed limit to make sure I wouldn't be tempted to snatch at the wheel again. The tires continued to nudge a little, so I decelerated to 40 and maintained that speed for the next mile. When the vehicle continued to pull, I lowered my speed to 35.

Why was the damned car pulling to the right?

Was it doing this on its own? Or was *I* the one doing it?

If I was the guilty party, wouldn't I be able to notice the moment I began putting the pressure on the wheel?

What if it was an unconscious act?

I thought about that for a moment and wondered what in heaven's name would make me unconsciously pull the car to the right...

Maybe you're doing this in a subconscious effort to avoid hitting the man you already hit...

That made no sense—none whatsoever.

Maybe not, but what else did I have that would explain this?

Nothing. Not a damned thing, actually...

Another sharp pull made me decrease my speed to 30, and when it pulled again, I knew I'd had enough. There was no other traffic around me, so I sped up to 50 and maintained this speed for the next mile...

Then I heard a strange voice.

Keep this up and you'll run over someone else, asshole...

I slammed on the brakes and pulled so quickly into the deserted tune-up place that I nearly T-boned into the lamp post on the left side of the entrance. For five minutes I just sat there, my heart hammering like a jackhammer, my nerves quivering as I struggled to come to grips with what just happened.

Had I heard someone's voice?

Was it my own? My conscience, perhaps? Or had my guilt emerged from the darkness of my thoughts to pound more harsh reality into my thick skull?

It sure as hell sounded like someone else's voice.

But how could that be? How could I possibly hear another voice? I was all alone in the car.

Suddenly suspicious, I flicked on the interior light with trembling fingers and forced myself to turn toward the back.

No one. I was just as alone as I'd been two minutes ago.

Still, that voice...it sounded so strange...

You're driving yourself crazy, dammit.

There. That was my own voice—I recognized it instantly.

But what about the other? Where had it come from? Whose was it? And why did I hear it the instant I'd accelerated to 50?

After sitting there a while longer, staring at the near-deserted highway and feeling like an idiot, I decided the damned voice didn't matter. The stress was getting to me. Lots of people heard voices when they were stressed. Lots of other people heard voices when they were scared or placed in extreme situations. I'd been through all three during the last few hours—how could I even question something like this?

I took a few deep breaths and told myself I'd be all right if I took it easy the rest of the way home. I was just a couple of miles from the condo—I could make it home standing on my head if I had to. I shouldn't even care if the car continued pulling to the right.

I edged back carefully onto Semoran. Keeping it at a steady 40, I made it the rest of the way without killing myself or destroying the car in the process.

The BMW pulled half a dozen more times, but I forced myself to ignore it. I wanted to get home and no longer cared about anything else.

Chapter 6

The hazy glow of the streetlamps gave the condo complex a look of eerie unfamiliarity.

By the time I pulled into my parking space in front of the two-story building, it was well past three in the morning, but I couldn't shake the feeling that I'd only been gone a couple of hours. I also couldn't shake the feeling that I didn't belong here. I suppose this was because my life had just been irrevocably transformed, and with these new changes, I no longer felt comfort or stability in a place that had been my home the last ten years of my life.

Life goes on…

That phrase had never meant much to me before. Just a few hours ago, a man's life had ended because of something I alone had done. Because of it, my own life could never be the same. All the while, the rest of the world slept undisturbed, unconcerned, and unmoved.

It just didn't seem fair. People were creatures of self-imposed isolation, separated by invisible walls and barriers shielding themselves from pain and anguish. Based on what had just happened to me, I realized that my own walls and barriers could only keep out so much.

When I finally decided to open the car door, I sensed that my walls and barriers had collapsed and would remain that way. And because I'd have to pass the front of the vehicle to venture up the concrete walk leading to the front entrance of my condo, my pain and anguish would continue. The very idea made me shudder in disgust.

Could I do it?

It didn't matter if I could or could not; I had to. If I wanted to go inside, I had to pass the front of the BMW.

Once again, I found that I was unable to move or even think of what I should do. For an instant I considered getting out, circling the back of the vehicle, walking down the street, calling a cab, and spending the night in a motel. That was a drastic move, but it was exactly how I felt.

I realized I was being silly. I was thirty-seven years old and suddenly afraid of getting out of my car and walking into my condo.

I needed to grow a pair. I was a mature adult in the prime of my life. I'd been on my own for nearly twenty years, so I really needed to get with the damned program.

The harsh words forced me out of my self-imposed insecurity. I had to face the fact that I'd have to look at the BMW sooner or later. Avoiding it would only make things worse.

"It's over and done with." I felt almost as if I was talking to someone else, but I found myself on a roll. "I killed a man. His worries are all over, and the police have absolved me of any blame. He shouldn't have been anywhere near that highway in his condition. There was no way in hell I could have avoided him or prevented the accident from happening."

But none of that mattered because I knew I couldn't absolve myself of the blame. I'd killed the man—nothing would ever change that. The fact that he'd been severely impaired seemed to make the situation even worse.

I had to snap out of this. To do so, I had to get out of the car and proceed up the walk. It was no big thing, really. In fact, it was something I'd done thousands of times before. Something I'd been able to do without any help whatsoever. Up until tonight, it had never been something I'd given much thought to.

However, the accident had made everything from that point on a brand-new experience. I'd plowed into a man on the highway. For all I knew, pieces of him could still be clinging to my car. And even if the damage was unnoticeable, the fact remained: my car had ended a human life and would never be the same again.

Like an automaton, I got out, closed the door behind me and shuffled up to the curb. I stepped up onto the walk and turned sharply, proceeding down the fifteen-foot stretch that veered to the left and would take me up to my front door. But just when I was about to pass the front of the BMW, I stopped suddenly and stood there, frozen, staring straight ahead, at the pine trees separating the buildings…and the dark shapes of the buildings beyond them…and the lights blinking behind the branches of the trees swaying lazily in the early morning breeze.

Keep going!

The voice was insistent. I knew I had to obey. I moved stiffly past the front of the car, turned left, and hurried the rest of the way up the walk, to the front door. As I struggled to get the key in the lock, an overwhelming urge to twist around and gawk at the BMW nearly overtook me, but I fought it down by getting the door open, bullying my way into the foyer, and slamming the door shut behind me.

For several minutes I stood with my back pressed against the door while waiting for my heart to stop thrashing. My inner voice kept telling me to keep my hand away from the doorknob so I wouldn't be tempted to open the door. Another voice urged me to go back down the walk and inspect the damage. I felt like I'd become two separate entities—that I'd turned into two people standing there. I knew it had to be my imagination, so I stayed right there and waited for the absurd urge to go away. There was no need to open the door or venture back outside, where some other new horror awaited me.

Once again, the entities tried taking over.

Open the door. You know you want to…

No. I really don't.

Just pull it open and have a quick look. It'll only take a moment…

No!

All you have to do is--

"Get the hell out of my head!"

The sudden silence told me I'd just killed the urge as well as the cursed voice in my head. Relieved, I closed my eyes and listened to the relaxing silence. When I was fairly certain the urge had scuttled back into the darkness where it belonged, I opened my eyes. This time, I found myself staring at the dimly lit foyer and wondering where I was.

It took me several moments to realize this was my home. My condo. My foyer. My own personal sanctuary. I didn't recognize it at first because too many things had happened during the last few hours, things that should never have happened. Things that had changed me forever.

How long had I been away from this place? Twelve hours? Fourteen? Or was it longer?

It didn't matter, did it? I was home.

As I entered the living room, that strange feeling that I'd been gone a long time came right back. It sounded bizarre, but I just couldn't shake it. The walls and furnishings looked unfamiliar. It was as if I'd never been here before—as if someone else lived here. Was this really my home? Was it the same place I'd left yesterday morning? The same place I'd been living when I started up Ellis & Associates?

Have a drink; you'll feel better…

At the time, I'd considered the cop's suggestion ludicrous. A cop suggesting I have a drink? Please… But now it sounded like a terrific idea. I immediately shuffled into the kitchen and grabbed a bottle of single malt Glenfiddich Scotch from the pantry, where I'd kept my booze since Laura and I split up two years ago. Wasn't that all the proof I needed that this was my place? If I knew where the booze was kept, wasn't that a good sign that I lived here?

Yes…but everything still felt strange, and so did I. To make matters worse, I feared I'd never be able to look at anything the same again.

I poured a couple of inches of Scotch into a glass, went back out into the living room and collapsed in the recliner. I had a sip of the stuff, lay back and closed my eyes. The strong malt warmed me, easing the tension from my limbs. I had another sip and tried to empty my mind, but the thoughts kept coming. I finished my drink, got up, went back into the kitchen, poured another two inches, went back into the living room, collapsed in the recliner once again and tried a second time to empty my mind. I just couldn't get the image of the accident out of my head.

I wanted more of my drink, but my body had suddenly gone numb, and I began growing warm as I melted into the firm fabric of the chair.

When I closed my eyes this time, a thick cloud of warm blackness enveloped me.

Chapter 7

The blackness cleared almost as quickly as it had appeared, and the first thing I saw was the BMW sitting in the middle of the road.

Traffic passed by without slowing down. I couldn't see any faces in the vehicles and suspected no one saw me or the car, either. It was as if I'd been transported to a different dimension. I didn't remember getting out of the car, but there I was, standing just a few feet away, gazing helplessly at the damage.

The front panel had obviously struck some large object. A dent the size of a football marred the surface, with blood covering a large portion of the paneling a few inches to the left, near the grille. As I stared, the blood began thickening. In just seconds, more blood had gathered, completely covering the front panel, bumper, hood, grille, and finally the windshield. Shiny splotches of dark-red peppered the roof.

The sight was incredible.

Where had all that blood come from? I vaguely remembered hitting someone, but the instant I tried recalling the details, everything turned hazy and dark. Then I heard footsteps behind me.

"You really did a job on me, man."

The strange voice made me jump as if I'd just been zapped with a cattle prod. I spun around.

A tall, slender figure dressed in black stood about five feet away. His clothes were stained in blood, his face and hands smeared with it as well. His hair and eyes were dark, but the blood covering his features prevented me from seeing his face. He gripped a black satchel tightly in the crook of his arm. It was also smeared with blood.

"Who…are *you*?" I asked, my voice a strained whisper.

"Who do ya think?"

My heart began pounding. My memory of the incident gradually cleared. I took an awkward step back. "You're *him*…aren't you?"

Grinning, he looked down at himself. Then he straightened. "Ya sure got *that* right. I'm certainly a *him*…"

"What I meant was—"

"I know what you meant, man. I was bein' what you'd call clever and spontaneous." He chuckled.

"Does that mean…are you—"

"I'm the dude you just splattered with your fancy ride." He jabbed a thumb at the BMW. "See there? Blood all over the damn place. Guess where it came from."

"I'm so…so *sorry*…" I began shaking. I wanted to get down on my knees and tell him just how badly I felt about all this and what this had done to me—how it had affected me. "I didn't mean…I really didn't mean to…to hit you…"

He chuckled. "Good thing ya didn't do it on purpose, then, huh?"

I didn't know what to say. He didn't *seem* angry, but I could feel the hatred emanating from his eyes and the heavy sarcasm in his tone. I couldn't blame him for the attitude. However, I couldn't ignore the compulsion to tell him what had been eating away at me since that fateful night. "You just...*walked right out in front of me*!"

He was silent for a little while. He seemed to be thinking it over. Then, after some thought, he said, "Yeah, I guess I did do that, didn't I?"

"Yes, you did."

He shrugged and grinned sheepishly. "Oops."

I ignored his mocking attitude. "Why'd you *do* it? Why'd you just *stand* there like that? Why didn't you at least *try* and get out of the way?"

He huffed. "I was totally wasted, man."

"But...you didn't *move*!" I just couldn't get that detail out of my head.

"Like I said, man, I was really wasted. Fucked up. I was havin' a moment—know what I mean?"

"No. I honestly don't..."

"It's like this... I was watchin' ya come at me, and it was really cool, man—I mean totally freaky and far out! I saw all these lights and then I saw you, and the lights turned all sorts of funky colors and began blendin' together, and then you were right there..."

"But why were you even *there*? Why'd you try and cross the street?"

"I was tryin' to get home."

"By walking?"

He laughed. "Ya sayin' I shoulda got in my ride and tried *drivin'* home?"

He definitely had a point.

"It's all right, dude. Don't sweat it. The cops cleared ya, didn't they?"

"That doesn't make it all right…"

He tilted his head. "Wanna *make* it all right?"

"I wish I could."

He lowered his voice. "All ya gotta do is find yourself one of those fancy time machines they've got in those old sci-fi flicks. When ya find one, just hop right in and go back in time, before this all happened. And when ya come at me the second time, you'll already know I'm gonna be there, so all ya gotta do is swerve out of the way—know what I mean?"

I stared at him and waited for him to laugh—to tell me he was kidding. He didn't. He seemed deadly serious.

"I can't. I wish I could, but I can't. I'm really sorry. I truly am."

"Like I said, don't sweat it. I know a lot of dudes that get high. I'm a musician. I never knew one that didn't get high. A lot of 'em tried doin' the time-travel thing when they were really strung-out, but they just couldn't cut it. Time travel's heavy-duty, dude. Most folks think it's impossible. Personally, I'm not quite sure where I stand on it. I'll let ya know if I ever find out."

Once again I ignored his attitude. "But I can't help feeling this way. I killed you, and I'll never forget that—not as long as I live!"

"It all comes out in the wash, man." He pulled the zipper down and opened the blood-stained satchel. The gleaming trumpet sat inside. He winked

55

at me as he pulled it out. I couldn't help noticing that it didn't appear damaged at all.

"It's not bent or anything?"

He turned it over in his hands. Then he held it close to his head, as if he was listening to it. He grinned. "Nope, the baby's just fine. I guess ya missed her, man. Good deal. Let's see if she still plays."

"She?"

"She's sleek and fancy and gets all warm and cuddly, and she'll do whatever you want her to do once you press your lips against her and handle her just right. She's definitely a lady." He nodded solemnly. "She's been my lady for years." He chuckled and patted it gently. "Guess who I sleep with at night, man…" He pulled a silver mouthpiece out of the satchel, screwed it into the main pipe then tucked the satchel in his left armpit. He watched me as he vigorously worked the valves. "Now she's primed and all ready to go…" He licked his lips, brought the horn up to his mouth and began playing an old jazz version of "*Summertime*," which I remembered from my father's vinyl collection. This man was really gifted, his tone rich, mellow and sweet. The melody flowed like warm molasses. He turned away and, still playing, walked down the street.

The darkness swallowed him up, but I still heard the song as the man and his silver-plated mistress vanished into a deep, lush silence.

Chapter 8

The buzzing of my cell phone awakened me.

It took me a few moments to collect myself. I rubbed my eyes and tried to clear my head. I soon discovered that I was sprawled on my recliner in the living room with a half-empty glass of Scotch in my lap.

I checked my clothes; they were dry. This puzzled me. Why hadn't I spilled the damned malt on myself? Had I slept that soundly? I couldn't even remember pouring the drink. I must have. No one else would have done it for me.

So why couldn't I remember?

I couldn't even recall if I'd slept at all. I remembered driving here and getting out of the car, but very little else.

Once I'd come in, I'd apparently poured a drink...

But had I actually *slept*?

And why was the song, "*Summertime*," echoing in my head?

If I hadn't slept, why would a song I hadn't heard in years—

The cell buzzed again.

I pulled it out of my pocket and flicked it on. The screen displayed Gloria's number at the office.

Why the hell was Gloria calling at this time of night? And what was she doing at the office?

Suddenly worried, I flicked it on.

"Gloria?"

"Brad? Is everything all right?"

"Gloria…what are you doing at the office at this hour?"

A pause. "I work here, Brad. So do you. What's going on? Why aren't you here?"

From the front window, the sun peeked in between the parted drapes. Panic struck me and I nearly dropped the cell as I brought up my left arm to gawk at my watch.

It was 9:45. My God. I must've fallen asleep on the recliner and just died. The last thing I remember was—

"Brad? Are you still there?"

"I'm here." I scrambled to get out of the recliner. It turned out to be a painful mistake. My legs were still asleep, and I collapsed as soon as I tried to stand. If it hadn't been for the arm of the recliner breaking my fall, I would have stumbled to the floor and cracked my head on the cocktail table.

I let myself fall back into the recliner and waited for my heart rate to settle down. Gloria was talking again, but I'd dropped the cell on the carpet during my stumble and couldn't hear what she was saying. I reached down and snatched it. "Gloria?"

"Brad? What's going on? Why aren't you here?"

That was a damned good question. Why was I still here, in my living room, wearing the same outfit I had on yesterday, when I'd left the office so late and—

Oh my God…

The events came back in a torrent.

Daniel Glen Morrison. The man who'd stepped out in front of my car...

An avalanche of dark, unpleasant images filled my head. I sat back and gripped the arms of the recliner to ride them out.

The drive home from the office. A man stepping in front of me in the middle of Colonial Drive. The loud thump. A black satchel flying in the air. The trip to the Police Station. Officer Silver. Detective Rossberg.

Daniel Glen Morrison. A tall, slender man of thirty who played jazz trumpet at local clubs...

He was gone. Dead. He was dead because I'd killed him.

He hadn't gotten out of the way because he'd been wasted and saw all sorts of funky colors and lights blending together only moments before I'd slammed into him—

I sat up sharply.

Colors? How the hell did I know about the colors?

Once again, haunting strains of "*Summertime,*" played beautifully and with great feeling by a mellow trumpet, filled my head.

An irritating buzzing sound emanated from my lap, and in an instant, "*Summertime*" was gone. Gloria was talking again.

I gawked at the phone in my lap. I'd dropped it there only a moment ago. Reluctantly I picked it up.

"Brad? *Please* tell me what's going on!"

"Gloria, something came up...I can't...I can't come in this morning."

Silence.

"Gloria? Did you hear me?"

"Brad, you've got that eleven o'clock. And, of course, the conference at one. The directors—"

"I can't come in!" I hadn't meant to shout, but the prospect of going to the office and dealing with those people made me nauseous. I lay back and closed my eyes.

"Brad? Are you all right?"

"No. Yes. I don't know. I just…can't come in."

"Are you sick?"

Sick was a good word. So was disgusted. Frustrated also fitted in quite nicely. But the fact remained: there was no way I could face anyone this morning, and surely no way I could make any rational decisions regarding the merger or anything else affecting Ellis & Associates. "I'm really not feeling well…"

A pause. "What do you want me to tell Chuck and Lois? You know they'll call you if you don't come in shortly…"

"Tell them I'm…under the weather."

Another pause. I could tell she was trying to figure out what was going on. Gloria didn't like it when something didn't make any sense. She wanted things to run smoothly. I couldn't blame her. Up until this moment, I'd felt just as she had.

"All right…I'll tell them you won't be coming in. They'll just have to reschedule the eleven o'clock. They'll be upset, but they'll have to get over it."

"Thanks, Gloria."

"Brad, I do wish you'd tell me what's going on. We *have* been working together a long time, you know. You can tell me anything. You should know that by now."

"I'll let you know what happened. I just can't tell you anything right now."

"Fair enough. I'll tell the directors you're not feeling well when they come in after lunch…"

"Do what you have to. I just can't come in today, and I can't tell you why. Not yet, anyway."

I hung up before she could say anything else. Then I forced myself out of the recliner and staggered to the bathroom. I suddenly had the overwhelming urge to throw up.

***

After a long, hot shower and several Tums, the nausea slowly began to subside.

I plodded into the kitchen to make a pot of coffee. I had no idea what I was going to do for the rest of the day, but I really didn't want to think too much about it. The evening seemed too distant and too ominous to even consider right now.

As the coffee brewed, I sat at the table and watched it until my eyes glazed over. As the billowing spurts of steam spiraled toward the ceiling, I tried making sense of what had gone wrong in my life and why it had all had unraveled before my eyes in a single night.

Was my divorce from Stacy responsible for any of this? The fact that she and I had parted on such bitter terms? Was part of all this the result of her ten-year-old daughter Nikki going through therapy when her mother and I began having our problems?

Was I still suffering guilt because I felt so badly for our divorce impacting Nikki's life? I'd purposely missed Nikki's all-star soccer match because her mother had upset me so much that I didn't want to attend at all, and my noticeable absence had hurt Nikki's performance considerably when she didn't see me cheering for her from the bleachers that day. Our relationship was never the same from that day on, and I'd never looked at myself in the same light again. To hurt and disappoint someone I cared so deeply about, over something that didn't even directly involve her, was something that scarred me much more than I'd ever imagined.

Had the act of ridding Nikki from my life let in a batch of self-hatred I wasn't even aware of?

Was my divorce from Laura something that enabled my self-loathing to grow and mature? Did it force me to spend more time at the office, prompting her to see a therapist and encouraging her to fall in love with him in the process? Did my problem have anything to do with the fact that she'd felt no remorse for her actions and blamed me for falling into the arms of another man?

Or was this miserable period of my life made even worse because I found that I honestly didn't care enough about our marriage to do whatever it took to keep it from crumbling?

Was it my obsession with work? With success? The long hours? The after-hours meetings? The countless times I'd slept in the office because I'd been too exhausted to drive home?

Had I made so much of a shambles of my life that I'd been much too distracted and too self-absorbed with my business affairs to watch where I was going or pay attention to what lay ahead of me on the highway?

Don't sweat it, dude…

I cringed in my chair.

Was that actually a strange voice in my head? Or my imagination stepping in to justify all this?

I began wondering once again if I'd had some bizarre dream when I'd first come home. Strangely, the instant I tried remembering, my mind went blank.

I considered myself much too young for memory lapses. I hadn't even been injured in the accident, but my memory betrayed me as if I'd just suffered a severe brain trauma.

Then, in the midst of my frustrations, that old song, "*Summertime*," filled my head again.

"This is really doing a number on me," I told myself.

I stiffened. That wasn't how I talked. Nor would I have said, "Don't sweat it, dude." I'd spoken this way in high school. Back then, everyone talked that way. But now I was the CEO and founder of a successful business. I had to act dignified and sound like I'd actually been to college.

I had to face the fact that what happened the night before had indeed done a number on me, and I could feel myself winding down in the process. I was hearing voices, suffering memory lapses and talking like a kid again. I was not only winding down, but I was also breaking up.

But even though I was totally aware of what was happening, I had no idea what to do about it. I was more concerned about fixing what happened than I was about fixing myself. I knew how absurd that sounded, but I just couldn't pull myself out of that mindset.

I honestly hoped there could be some way out of this.

"All ya gotta do is find yourself one of those fancy time machines they've got in those old sci-fi flicks. When ya find one, just hop right in and go back in time, before this all happened. And when ya come at me the second time…"

That voice again. But this time, instead of agonizing over what it was and where it was coming from, I found that I was stressing over the message itself. It sounded simple in theory. And it was. The problem was that unless someone came up with a foolproof way of time-travel, I was just going to have to live the rest of my life carrying around the devastating guilt that I'd killed a fellow human being.

It was time to have some coffee. I poured a cup, added sugar and went into the living room. Then I sat down in the recliner and flicked on the widescreen. The local news came on with the story of a local musician being run down on Colonial Drive. Just as the anchor began talking about the victim, known in local jazz circles as Danny Glen, the lead player in the Bits of Jazz four-piece combo, I flicked it off and tossed the remote onto the sofa. Then I put my coffee mug on the end table, got up and started pacing.

"I can't take this anymore," I told the room. "This is killing me."

Go back in time, dude...

"I can't. I wish I could, but I can't!"

Don't sweat it...

"How the hell am I supposed to—"

I stopped pacing. For nearly a minute I just stood there, listening to the silence. Then I began looking around.

Who was I talking to? Whose voice was I hearing? And why did I think I'd heard all this before?

The sorrowful strains of "*Summertime*" echoed in my head again.

"Dammit!" I needed some other tune in my head—something that would drown out this song and keep me distracted for a little while.

I opened the stereo cabinet and randomly pulled out an album. I flicked on the turntable, removed the LP from its paper sleeve and laid it carefully onto the turntable. I lifted the needle, lowered it gently onto the surface of the spinning album and made sure the volume was on medium.

The music began playing. I cringed.

It turned out to be one of my father's old Harry James albums, with Harry playing the lead solo in the opening song, "*Summertime.*"

65

I backed up. Was this really happening? What was the significance of that song? More importantly, how did I pick it out so easily? There were more than a hundred albums in that cabinet—how could I possibly know which one I was going to pick? I'd grabbed the first one I touched—why did it have to be an album with *"Summertime"* as the opening number?

I snuck back to the stereo as if a poisonous snake was lurking inside and turned the volume all the way down. Then I switched off the stereo and backed away again.

Would it continue playing?

It's off, brainiac… It can't *play anymore…*

Who was I talking to now? Myself? Or that strange voice again?

Did it matter?

The only thing that did matter was that damned song.

I stared at the stereo, my heart pounding as I waited for the song to start up again.

The silence continued.

Somewhat relieved, I flicked on the widescreen again but steered clear of the local news stations. Fortunately, Turner Classic Movies was showing an old John Wayne Western.

Nothing threatening about that, was there?

I collapsed on the sofa, closed my eyes, and instantly fell asleep.

Chapter 9

I opened my eyes to total darkness.

Trembling, I gazed at it, waiting for it to clear—to vanish and reveal what lay beyond it. It remained black and still—as if it was nothing but pure emptiness.

Frightened and confused, I began moving forward, holding my arms out in front of me in case I bumped into something. I moved slowly and stiffly, my feet barely rising above the hard, uneven ground. The blackness heightened my fear that I might trip over something or fall into a bottomless abyss.

I continued shuffling forward, moving just a couple of inches at a time. My arms were getting tired, but I struggled to keep them out in front of me. I hoped that I'd eventually connect with something and that the darkness would gradually thin out or disappear entirely.

The distant sound of a trumpet penetrated the heavy silence. It was playing a beautiful ballad and brought tears to my eyes.

I immediately lowered my arms, closed my eyes and listened. After about a minute or so, the trumpet stopped playing and was replaced with stringed instruments. Soon after, a chorus of beautiful voices came in.

It was the most haunting ballad I'd ever heard.

"It's *"Trumpeter's Prayer"*," said a voice quite close to me.

I opened my eyes. The darkness had dimmed. A man's face appeared. The man I'd accidentally killed stood just a few feet from me, grinning and cradling his trumpet in his arms as the voices and the strings continued performing the ballad.

"It's a beautiful piece," I whispered. "I don't think I've ever heard anything quite as haunting."

"It was recorded by Conrad Gozzo in the early sixties." The man's expression had turned solemn.

"I don't think I've ever heard of him," I said.

"Are you a trumpet player?"

"No…"

"Then you've never heard of him. The Goz was the best—the absolute greatest of lead horn players. This song was written especially for him when he was at his peak."

"What happened to him?" I asked, suddenly curious.

Danny Glen remained solemn. "Goz liked his food and his booze. He had gout, diabetes, and cirrhosis. And since he was kind of on the hefty side, his heart wasn't in great shape, either. He was a mess. He was only forty-two when he died." He shook his head. "But no one could top him when it came to playin' that trumpet."

"Not even you?"

He blinked but said nothing.

I shrugged. "I couldn't help noticing how terrific you play. Your tone…it's so mellow, so smooth, so—"

"Not even me," he said finally. "Maybe in a few years…" Then he smiled, and his laughter

68

echoed in the darkness. "I forgot. You kinda put an end to that, didn'tcha, sport?"

I had nothing to say. I couldn't believe it was possible, but I felt even worse than ever.

He shrugged. "Like I told ya before, don't sweat it."

"But I didn't mean to—"

"I know ya didn't."

"If I could, I'd go back in time—"

"I know, but ya can't."

"There must be *some*thing I can do…"

"Maybe…" He looked down at his horn and began rubbing the rim of his mouthpiece with his thumb. He appeared deep in thought.

"Maybe?" I couldn't help wondering what he was thinking.

He nodded. "Ya seem sincere, dude."

"I am. I really and truly am."

He went silent again, staying that way for about a minute. Then he winked. "Then I'm pretty sure you'll find some way of squarin' us."

"But how?"

He shrugged. "Maybe it'll come to ya one day, but if it doesn't, don't get your panties in a wad over it. Like I keep tellin' ya, don't sweat it. It was an accident. As they say, accidents happen." Then he raised his horn to his lips and turned around. A moment later, he began walking away slowly, playing the rest of the song.

The darkness thickened, and the blackness swallowed him up.

***

A cluster of bright lights killed the darkness.

I covered my eyes to keep the glare away. When I lowered my hands, I found that I was lying on my living room sofa. My watch said that it was slightly before dinnertime. When my empty stomach protested loudly, only then did it occur to me that I hadn't eaten in a long while.

I got up stiffly. Had I zoned out? Or had I experienced another dream? As before, as soon as I tried bringing it back, my mind went blank. It was probably one of those bizarre, pointless dreams I'd had in the past that made no sense.

From the widescreen, Turner was playing something from the Forties with Gene Tierney. I'd always considered Tierney one of Hollywood's all-time hottest babes, but I just wasn't in the mood for a movie. I shuffled into the kitchen and made a roast beef and Swiss cheese sandwich on rye. I grabbed a beer, sat down at the table, and picked up my sandwich. It looked good, but I soon discovered that I just wasn't hungry, so I put it back on the plate and picked up the beer. I took a healthy gulp from it and immediately scolded myself for drinking on an empty stomach, but since I wasn't very hungry, I kept the scolding short.

A few minutes later, my stomach protested again, this time louder. I picked up the sandwich and bit into it. It tasted good, so I had more of it and washed it down with another slug of beer.

It didn't take me very long to finish the sandwich. After I got up and washed off the plate, I realized I was restless and needed to get out of the condo.

I went down the hall. My cell buzzed; I pulled it out of my pocket. It was Chuck Finley, one of my partners. I didn't want to talk to him or anyone else about business. I knew full well that, given my present mood, I couldn't keep my mind on anything for very long. I pocketed the cell and let it go to voicemail. Then I went into the bedroom, changed into something casual and comfortable and went back out into the living room.

Then I realized I'd have to face the BMW.

You've got to get over this.

I know.

You can't continue acting like a frightened rabbit the rest of your life.

I know that, too.

Step outside, march down that walk and face that car like a man!

My conscience—or whatever had been trying to talk sense into me—was absolutely right. Gathering up what little courage I could find, I shuffled down the walk and stopped ten feet short of my beloved BMW, which, up until this moment, had been my pride and joy. For more than a minute I just stood there, staring at the gleaming windshield.

Don't be a coward. Lower your eyes.

Give me time.

You've had more than enough of that, so stop making excuses!

Once again, the voice was right. It was extremely important that I do this. If I didn't, I should just scurry back inside, lie down on the bed and wait to die. That would surely be the coward's way out.

Suddenly ashamed of myself, I struggled to clear my mind of all distractions. Then, focusing on the task at hand, I lowered my gaze to the front panel.

The sight took me by surprise. I took three cautious steps closer. Then I gasped.

There was no evidence of anything that would even suggest a full-grown man had slammed into it. There was nothing visible on the panel...or grille...or even the front bumper. No blood stains. No flesh or evidence of tissue or clothing. No bumps or dents in the body itself. If I didn't know better, I would've sworn nothing had ever touched this vehicle.

The man I'd plowed into and killed had left no visible evidence that his body had even touched the front of my car...

Chapter 10

After standing there like a zombie for what felt like half an hour, I snapped out of my fugue state, went back inside and called the Orlando Police Department.

I asked to speak with Officer Silver. I didn't know if he'd be able to tell me anything; I just felt that I should try and find out if such a thing was possible, or if I was just imagining it. I was tempted, if only briefly, to take another stroll out front but quickly talked myself out of it. If I saw anything different the second time around, I'd freak out.

But before I did anything, I wanted to talk to Silver and find out if what I'd just seen was indeed possible.

After waiting on hold for nearly five minutes, I heard a click, and his voice came on. "This is Officer Silver speaking. Who am I talking to?"

"This is Brad Ellis. Do you remember me?"

"Of course I do, Mr. Ellis. Everything okay?"

"No, sir. Something just came up that I can't explain, and I desperately need to talk to someone about it."

A pause. "Does this concern what happened on Colonial Drive last night?"

"Yes."

"All right, then…if you've got more questions—"

"Officer, do you know if anyone checked out my car after the accident?"

"Sir?"

"Did anyone actually check it out? Look at it? Inspect it for damage?"

"Well, I'd have to find the file to see what was written in the accident report—"

"Did you happen to notice the front of my car when you first walked up to it?"

"I was much too busy trying to determine if you were drunk or needed medical attention. Once I reached your door, I admit that I was concentrating only on you, and—"

"Officer, I just inspected my car. I looked at it just half an hour ago."

"Okay…"

"There's nothing on it."

Another pause. "What exactly are you trying to tell me?"

"There's not one mark on my car. Not even a smudge or blemish. No dents anywhere. No blood. If I didn't know better, I'd say nothing came into contact with my car last night."

Silence.

I couldn't believe he had nothing to say. He was either as bumfuzzled as I was or doing his best to keep from saying anything that might worsen this. I'd seen enough cop shows and heard about cover-ups. I just didn't see the need for anything to be covered up in this case. I didn't think Daniel Glen Morrison was in politics, a Fed, or an undercover detective. As far as I knew, he was simply a jazz musician.

"Doesn't that sound odd to you?" I asked.

"Mr. Ellis—"

"I ran into another human being. I flung him in the air like a rag doll, and when he landed, he slammed into hard pavement and died."

"I know what you must be feeling right now—"

"I don't think you do."

"Then tell me."

"There should be a mark. A dent. A scratch. Some blood, at least. What I'm trying to say is that there should be tangible evidence that I actually *killed* someone!"

"Mr. Ellis, I'm sure you know that this sort of thing isn't an exact science. No accident is. We can't bring along a slide rule to an accident scene, write down clean measurements and coordinates and use them to figure out exactly what happened. There weren't even any security cameras recording activity in the immediate area that we could've used to review the accident in detail. In this case, we had to go by your testimony alone and, judging by the physical evidence—"

"Don't you think there should be some evidence showing on my vehicle that clearly shows I murdered someone?"

"You didn't *murder* anyone. You—"

"Whatever you want to call it, don't you think there should be at least a trace or fragment of evidence that demonstrates something actually happened to my car when I ran into the man?"

"Why should there be?"

I was getting more frustrated by the second. "There's nothing to indicate I even *hit* the poor man!"

"Mr. Ellis, as you just said, he was tossed in the air. When he landed, he cracked the back of his skull on the macadam. The blunt force trauma to the back of his head substantiates this, and—"

"But I *hit* him! My car slammed *into* him!"

"You don't know *how* you hit him. It was quite possibly a glancing blow that killed him the moment he landed. As I recall at the morgue, both knees were shattered. This suggests your bumper served as the point of initial contact. It hit him and flung him. He might have been tossed over the roof of the vehicle, for all we know. In other words, the bumper might have been his only contact with your vehicle—which should tell you why there wouldn't be a mark anywhere else on the car."

I didn't know what to say to that. It made sense, but it certainly didn't make me feel any better.

"Mr. Ellis, you've been through a horrific experience. I suggest that you try your best to put it all behind you."

"Now how the hell am I supposed to do that?"

"Try to convince yourself that you couldn't have avoided it. All evidence indicates that the man himself made the tragedy inevitable. He stepped right out in front of your car. Instead of trying to get out of the way, he didn't move. For all we know, he might have done this on purpose."

"On *purpose*?" That possibility had never occurred to me.

"People do it all the time."

"You mean suicide?"

"That's exactly what I mean. They step out in traffic…or in front of trains…or do headers from buildings. Many of them create situations where we have to actually shoot them. People are troubled, Mr. Ellis. You know this as well as I do. Many folks just can't cope with what life has dealt them. Many are mentally sick…or troubled…or going through some terrible trauma they just can't deal with."

I didn't know what to say.

"Mr. Ellis…you know what I'm talking about, don't you?"

"I *think* I do…"

"You sound doubtful."

"That's probably because I am."

"You don't think the man could have stepped out in front of you on purpose?"

"No."

"Why not?"

I'd been getting some sort of eerie feeling about Daniel Glen Morrison and strongly suspected that he wasn't the sort of person to attempt suicide as a way out. He'd been drunk and he'd done coke, but I just couldn't believe he'd deliberately stepped in front of my car to end his own life.

"I just don't think he did. He was a jazz musician. A terrific trumpet player."

A pause. "You *knew* him?"

"No…"

"Then how do you know anything about him?"

"The satchel. It contained a trumpet."

77

"That doesn't necessarily mean he was a terrific player..."

"He played for a living."

"That still doesn't mean—"

"He was terrific, dammit. I heard him. He had great potential." I couldn't believe the things I was saying or how I knew what I was talking about. I only knew that for some strange reason, I found that I was unable to consider that the man I'd killed was anything but a great musician. "He would've been one of the best if I hadn't...if I hadn't...if he hadn't died last night."

"Mr. Ellis, I don't know what's going on, but I can tell you're taking this much too hard. You need to put this behind you."

"I honestly don't know if I can."

"If you don't, it'll eventually destroy you. I've seen people just like you take something like this to heart and find themselves under the care of a psychiatrist. I've also seen people bypass the shrink and head right off to the rubber room to spend the rest of their days on heavy meds."

I had nothing to say to that.

"Mr. Ellis, you're a very nice, honorable man. I don't want to see anything happen to you. If you need to talk to a professional let them try and help you. Use your company's health plan and go that route or give me another call and I'll see if I can possibly refer you to someone I've come across in my police work. In any event, you have to survive this. As far as I know, it's your only option."

Chapter 11

"You have to survive this…"

I spent the next hour on the sofa with the cop's words running through my head like some ethereal message from the dead. The widescreen was on, but I wasn't paying attention. I could only think of Silver's possible suicide theory. Regardless of what he'd said, I knew Morrison had not committed suicide. As I'd told Silver, I didn't know how I knew—just that I did.

Each time I caught myself entertaining that theory, something told me otherwise. I didn't know Morrison, but each time I thought of him intentionally stepping in front of my car, the idea seemed totally absurd.

But how could I know for sure? The only thing I did know about him was that he'd played jazz trumpet in local clubs and was totally drunk and zoned out on coke when I ran into him. Other than that, I knew nothing.

So how did I know he wouldn't have purposely stepped in front of my car? And how did I know he was a terrific player with a lot of potential?

Regardless, I found myself struggling hard once again to sort it out…to make sense of the fact that I'd killed a man but could not see any evidence of it.

It occurred to me that this could be a blessing in disguise. If I *had* seen evidence of the man's blood, tissue or clothing on my car, things would be much worse. The sight would have destroyed me. I probably would have thrown up or fainted. I would have nightmares about it for months and would not be able to get the image out of my head.

The BMW would have to go. Even if I'd paid someone to pick it up, take it away and detail it until it gleamed like polished gems, I'd continue to see the evidence in my head. I could never drive that car again.

But I *hadn't* seen anything at all, and this was tormenting me.

What was wrong with me? Why was it so important to see physical evidence of the man I'd killed? Was I searching for some way of justifying all this? Would it help me make sense of what I'd done? Would a smear of blood or chunks of brain matter make this more tolerable? Would I be able to sleep better if I'd seen a dent on the BMW? Would a scratch in the metal make life better and more pleasant for me?

After struggling through this nonsense for more than an hour, I realized that the issue would never be resolved this way. I had to squeeze out of this self-imposed cocoon I'd created, get some air, and give my brain a well-deserved rest. The condo was smothering me.

The urge to get in the car and drive to unwind had been growing steadily. I sensed an overwhelming need to be somewhere else. A nice, comfortable bar would help me relax. There were several lounges on Semoran that catered to the quieter, more mature crowd—some providing soothing dinner music, others featuring small combos that played the classic romantic stuff.

I checked my wallet for cash, grabbed my keys, squirmed into my lightweight jacket, and hurried to the front door. I pulled it open and froze.

Vera Hobson was standing on the front stoop, smiling at me. She wore a red sleeveless V-necked tee shirt, form-fitting designer jeans and cream-colored open-toed pumps. She clutched the thick strap of her leather handbag with her left hand and the neck of a bottle of champagne with her right. Her thick red hair swept heavily over her shoulders. She looked fabulous.

And she was the last person I wanted to see.

"Calm down, Brad," she said, smiling brightly. "I didn't expect a brass band...but can't you at least show me the hint of a smile to give me the illusion that you're maybe a *little* happy to see me?"

I could tell she was trying to joke about my cold reaction. I hated myself for not appearing sociable, but my urge to get away hadn't diminished at all.

Get rid of her.

My inner voice had a valid point, but I had to tread lightly. Vera was a very intelligent, pleasant woman, and I'd been comfortable with her since we started seeing one another. But this was a new relationship, and I couldn't be rude to her. After all, she'd come all the way from South Conway to visit me. In rush hour traffic, that translated into thirty, perhaps forty-five minutes. Telling her to go away

81

would be totally unfair. It was also something I'd never done to anyone before.

You don't want to see her now.

Maybe not, but I still have to do this without hurting her feelings, or—

"Aren't you gonna ask me in?"

"I'm sorry." I stepped aside. "C'mon in."

She slipped past me very close, and a sensation of lavender and vanilla brushed my face. As I closed the door, I struggled with all sorts of excuses I could use to bow out of this. When I turned, she held out the bottle. "I hope you don't mind. I figured since you've been working so hard lately, you might appreciate some relaxing bubbly." She gave me a quick once-over. "You look like you're going out."

I suddenly realized that now would not be a good time to tell her I was going to a bar. "I needed groceries. I was just going out to pick up a few things. No big deal."

She smiled. "Then you won't mind if we have some bubbly?"

Get rid of her, that cursed voice repeated.

Just as I tried once more to figure out some way of bowing out of this gracefully, she came right over, wrapped her arms around my waist, pressed against me and kissed me passionately. When she broke away, she whispered, "Let's go to bed first and have the bubbly later on—but only if we need it."

"Vera…"

"C'mon, now. It'll relax you…eventually."

82

I just sighed.

She kissed me again. Then she began kissing my neck. Despite my original intentions, I realized that I was getting aroused as well. She obviously wanted sex, and I discovered that I wanted it just as much as she did.

Forget it. Tell her you're tired and don't feel well.

This is probably just what I need right now...

She kissed me again. "Let's go to the bedroom," she whispered. "I love your couch, but in my present mood, I'll need a lot more room to move around…"

"Now?"

Her large green eyes grew. "Yes. Right now."

Chapter 12

It didn't take either of us very long to realize I was unable to perform. Just minutes after several clumsy attempts on my part to initiate the festivities, Vera turned on her side and frowned. "Tell me what's wrong, Brad."

I collapsed beside her and struggled to decide what I should tell her. We'd only been on three dates. They'd all gone well, but I really didn't know the lady very well. I knew she was divorced, ran a hair salon in Orlando and lived by herself in a beautiful two-story condo in South Conway. Other than that, we were practically strangers. We'd been getting along very well, but I just couldn't imagine sharing this horror with someone I'd known only a couple of weeks.

"It's me, isn't it?" she finally asked.

"No. It's definitely *not* you…"

She pushed some hair away from her face. "I was too bold, wasn't I? Most guys don't like a girl climbing all over them. I learned that years ago, when I first started dating, but obviously forgot all about it. Guys prefer initiating everything. I can't say as I blame them, although it's very frustrating, waiting for the guy to make the first move—especially when the girl finds him so attractive." She gave me a searching look. "You're obviously one of those guys, aren'tcha?"

"No. It isn't that at all."

"What *is* it, then?"

"Vera…"

"You can tell me. I'm tough. I can take it."

I touched her cheek. "It isn't you. I mean that. I like you, Vera. And I honestly don't mind it one bit if you decide to take the initiative."

"I've been around the block, Brad. You knew that coming in. I'm thirty-four, for God's sake. In female years, that's more like forty, maybe even forty-five. I've been married and divorced. I've had two miscarriages. My last boyfriend drained nearly half the money from my checking account before I found out. Whatever's going on with you, I'll understand. I know you've been around the block, too. I just don't want us keeping things from one another—especially at this stage. I think we could be starting something that might actually turn out very good, and—"

"I'm going through something right now, Vera. It's really bad, believe me."

"Is it a work thing? That merger you told me about?"

"It has nothing to do with—" Just then, I realized that she'd just given me an opportunity to get out of this without actually telling her what was really going on.

"With what, Brad?"

"The merger…it's eating me up inside. It's obviously taking a lot out of me, and it's dragging on entirely too long."

"What did you just mean when you said—"

"I was just trying to say that it has nothing to do with you at all." I got up and grabbed my housecoat from the chair. I shrugged into it, furious with myself for treating her like this. She'd bought a bottle of champagne and drove across town, expecting to enjoy a pleasant evening with me. But it just couldn't be helped. After all, what I was going through wouldn't be something the average woman would want to be part of, and I couldn't blame her if she decided to call it quits.

She didn't deserve any of this. She was a tremendous lady and I considered myself lucky to have stumbled onto her. But this was something I couldn't possibly share with anyone—especially someone I'd known only a couple of weeks.

"Tell me, Brad." She sat up, revealing her magnificent breasts. Under other circumstances, I would have wasted no time pouncing on her. But right now, sex was the farthest thing from my mind. "*Please* tell me what you're going through."

"It's the pressure. The meetings. It's coming home so exhausted that I can't even think straight. It's getting phone calls at ten and eleven at night. It's…it's getting to be too damned much." Even with the a/c running, it was getting uncomfortably warm in the room. I went to get a drink from the pantry in the kitchen. As I was pouring two inches of Scotch into a glass, I felt her coming up behind me. She'd put on her jeans and was squeezing into her tee shirt.

"Pour one for me, too, please?"

I got another glass, poured and then dropped a cube in it, as she preferred. She took it and went over to the table. She watched me as I sat down facing her and continued watching me as she sipped. Then she put her glass down. "Tell me what I can do, Brad. I really need to know."

I took a sip of my drink and stared at the glass while wondering how I could get her to leave without upsetting her too much. My mind was going berserk, coming up with all kinds of wild ideas. She already had an idea of what was happening at the office. Since I'd mentioned the merger to her, she could guess that I wasn't quite myself. I just wasn't sure if she considered it serious enough to cause me to turn away from her even after she'd taken off all her clothes and initiated enough passion to excite any normal healthy man. Anyone with any sense—especially an intelligent, attractive woman—would suspect that any normal guy who could resist sex at that particular moment was either impotent or deeply troubled. And since I'd already proven to her that I wasn't impotent, this left her with the only other conclusion.

"The merger should be wrapped up in a couple of weeks," I told her. Then I lifted my glass and had another sip. "If I can survive the next two weeks, I think I'll be able to manage. I might even be able to wind down and start enjoying myself again."

"Then you're saying you don't want me to do anything? You just want me to…to wait until this thing resolves itself?"

"I wouldn't blame you if you decided to tell me to go to hell and then leave."

"What kind of girl would I be if I did something like that?"

I shrugged. "Practical? Sensible?"

She laughed. "I've never been accused of being either."

"As I said, I wouldn't blame you if you were."

"Stress can be a killer, all right. I should know. I deal with the public all the time. People can be real assholes—especially women."

I nodded and sipped more Scotch.

Killer…

Maybe you need to tell her about the killer in this room…

I put the glass down rather shakily.

"Brad?"

I stared at my glass and waited for my heart to stop pounding so loudly. My imagination. It was just my imagination. It was my own voice talking. My guilt. My thoughts.

What else could it have been?

"Are you all right?"

The voice had no doubt been my own conscience. It was scolding me once again for what happened. Nothing else made sense.

"Brad?"

"I think so…" I tried sounding normal but wasn't sure I could manage after hearing something like that coming out of my own mind.

"I can tell you're really uncomfortable."

Growing warm again, I opened my robe a couple of inches. "I'm just a little warm."

"Brad, you really need to start taking care of yourself."

"I know."

"It's easier said than done, isn't it?"

I nodded.

We sat in silence for a few minutes, gazing at one another.

Vera finished her drink. Then she got up. "I think I'd better be getting a move on."

"You're leaving?"

"You don't want me here with you tonight." She placed a hand on my shoulder and squeezed it, then went out into the hall.

Despite all this awkwardness, I found that I was greatly relieved. Vera was right; I didn't want her with me tonight. I didn't want anyone with me tonight. The urge to get out of this condo hadn't stopped growing even after Vera had come to the door. In fact, it had grown even more urgent during the last couple of minutes.

She came back down the hall, forcing a comb through her hair. I got up and followed her into the living room, where she picked up her handbag from the sofa. "I guess we'll have to do a rain check." She studied my face. "That is, unless you don't want one…"

"Of course I want one. We still have to tap that bubbly, don't we?"

Smiling, she rubbed my cheek. "Will you call me tomorrow? I need to know what's going on, and I really want you to start feeling better."

"If anyone can help with that, it would be you."

She smiled. "Give me more of a chance the next time, okay?"

"I'll call you."

"Promise?"

"Of course."

She kissed me lightly and turned for the door.

"Vera?"

"Yes?" She turned.

"I'll be all right in a few days."

"I know."

"I just need...I—"

"I know what you need, Brad. You just don't want it right now."

I smiled sheepishly.

"You won't forget that rain check, will you?"

I shook my head. "Not in *this* lifetime."

She pulled open the door and left.

I watched her as she got in her Honda, waved, and backed out of her space. As she drove away, I went back to the bedroom, changed, and got ready to leave.

Chapter 13

Not long after I got in the BMW, I discovered that the drive down Semoran Boulevard was about to become frightening.

Things turned weird the moment I pulled onto the main stretch and joined the southbound traffic. Each time I stopped at a red light, I experienced the overpowering urge to drive straight ahead, even though I'd originally wanted to turn down Old Cheney, which led to the Crestview Lounge. The BMW seemed to have a mind of its own. Despite my efforts to turn at the light, I kept going straight, until I'd reached the intersection of Semoran and Colonial Drive.

Once I made the right on Colonial, the BMW continued going straight, just as it had on Semoran. Some weird invisible force seemed to be directing me, and even though I tried several times to pull into one of the strip malls or restaurants along the way, I found that I had no choice but obey whatever force had been directing me west.

Two blocks from the intersection of Colonial and Semoran, I passed the area where the accident had taken place. My heart fluttered and my hands clutched the wheel in a death grip as I approached the next intersection. Thankfully, the light stayed green. I rushed through and kept so close to the Lexus in front of me that I nearly tapped its rear bumper.

As I zipped through the intersection, I forced myself to keep staring at the Lexus. However, my eyes wandered, shifting to my side mirror. For one brief agonizing instant I thought I saw someone standing in the middle of the intersection several car lengths behind me. Then I blinked. The figure vanished and I knew it was just my imagination.

It took me another block or so before I could settle back in my seat and restore circulation in my hands. I told myself to relax. The unpleasant moment had passed, and I'd survived.

Twenty minutes later, when I'd reached the hectic intersection of Colonial and 441, I felt that the BMW wanted to turn left. Instead of continuing to fight the wheel, I let it do as it wished, and in moments we were heading south. Traffic remained heavy, the stores, plazas and restaurants filled, the parking lots chaotic.

Several intersections later, the BMW began edging toward the right. We crossed two lanes and made a right onto a secondary road that went straight for about a quarter of a mile, until the car slowed, turned onto a narrow dirt road and, about half a mile later stopped in front of a dirty gray stone building with the lighted sign, *Raymond's,* winking erratically above the arched doorway.

The tired-looking old building had the look of quiet loneliness, but the five cars and four pickups parked in the gravel lot out front told me otherwise. The two front windows showed evidence of light behind the blinds, but the absence of heavy throbbing, which normally came from a bar doing a thriving business, suggested that it might be the quiet place I'd been looking for. I eased up to the space at the end and put the BMW in park. Then I sat back and tried analyzing what had actually happened.

I couldn't even remember driving here, nor could I recall where I was. I'd wanted to stop on Old Cheney Highway and have a drink at the closest and quietest lounge I could find. But for some strange reason, my *car* had different ideas.

Although I wasn't exactly sure where I'd come, I knew this wasn't the Crestview, nor was it just a mile or so from my complex. And it certainly didn't look like any lounge I'd ever been to before.

Go on in...

That same mysterious voice that had been interfering with my thoughts since the accident interrupted them again, this time telling me the obvious. I knew I should go in, but I just couldn't help feeling skeptical about all this and somewhat frightened about the situation itself. I couldn't shake the strong feeling that I'd *been brought* here, although that concept seemed ridiculous.

If my feeling was correct, what *was* it that had brought me here? Why did I keep thinking my car had been responsible?

That seemed preposterous. How could an inanimate object possess such powers?

Was it some unseen force? How could something I wasn't even sure I believed in possess the power to take me to some place I didn't even know existed? I hadn't wanted to come to this section of town in the first place and saw no logical reason why I'd ended up here. But I *had* come here, and all I could surmise was that something I couldn't quite figure out at the moment had, for some unknown reason, brought me here against my wishes.

As I continued to sit behind the wheel, I tried to come up with some explanation that might make sense of this. But after several frustrating minutes, I realized nothing would come to me.

Don't stress yourself. Just go inside and have your drink. You'll feel better.

Sighing tiredly, I pushed open the door and got out.

***

I heard no music or laughter when I stepped inside.

I wondered, for a moment, if the place was an actual bar. The foyer was small, dark, and deserted. A large wooden podium and a couple of chairs hugged the wall on my left, but the area was deserted, and there was no hostess in sight to greet me. A dozen or so metal hooks protruded from the wall facing me, but no coats or jackets hung from them. Curious, I slipped through the archway straight ahead.

A large, dimly lit room filled with maybe forty or so small empty round tables loomed in front of me. A long rectangular bar extended from the wall on my right. Nearly a dozen people sat on stools in front of it, drinking and chatting away.

94

There was no music. I heard only whispering, laughter and the clinking of glasses. A jukebox huddled in dark silence in the far corner, about ten feet from the other end of the bar. I didn't think it was even plugged in.

At the opposite end of the large room, four people sat at a table next to the piano, which had been shoved against the wall next to the small circular stage. Three were males; the fourth, a female. They all seemed young—perhaps in their mid- or late twenties. The woman was very slender, with long dark brown hair. She wore jeans and a maroon windbreaker and slumped forward, her elbows on the table. Her hair extended to within a foot of the floor, hiding her shoulders. The others slumped forward as well. None of them spoke; all four appeared to be meditating. Two bottles of beer, three shot glasses and a can of Sprite were grouped close together in the center of the table.

Something rested on top of the piano. I couldn't tell what it was from where I was standing. The area was slightly darker than the bar. The main source of light came from a couple of small overhead dome sights. The light closest to the piano was perhaps twenty feet from it, leaving much of the area in shadow. From where I stood, it looked like some sort of suitcase, or overnight bag—

"You wanna drink? Or do ya just wanna stand there and admire the place?"

Some chuckling.

The barman, big and broad-shouldered, with a dark brush cut and tattoos covering his large, hairy forearms, watched me from behind the bar counter. He looked ex-military. The twitch in his left eyelid suggested that he probably wasn't the world's most patient individual.

I sat on the end stool. "I'll have Scotch. No ice."

He went back to the bar.

I shifted on my stool and went back to watching the foursome at the other end of the room. They hadn't moved and appeared to be staring at the table. Since they were at least forty feet away, I couldn't see their faces, but their body language suggested grief. Some tragedy had obviously shaken them.

"Here ya go." The barman placed the glass on a napkin in front of me. I handed him a five. He took it and went back to the register. I sipped, put the glass back down onto the napkin and turned back to the foursome.

Every once in a while the girl raised her head and turned toward the piano. Then she turned back to the table and wiped her eyes with a Kleenex. The others were sneaking glances at the piano as well.

I caught myself staring at it, wondering what was lying on top of it. For an instant I thought I had it, but as soon as I did, a cold wave sliced through me, and I turned away. Suddenly I couldn't look at it. I suspected what it was and knew that if I was right, I could never look at it again…

The satchel. It had to be the satchel I'd seen lying in the middle of the road. If it was, the foursome sitting over there…they had to be—

Plain enough for you, dude? the cursed voice asked me.

Another sheet of ice sliced through me, and I nearly lost my balance. Steadying myself, I groped for my drink. My shaking fingers almost dropped the glass on its short trip to my mouth. I had to use both hands to steady it.

"You okay?" The barman was watching me.

I carefully lowered the glass and was somehow able to place it back onto the napkin without dropping it. My pulse raced. I had to swallow a couple of times to get the words out. "What happened...what's going on...over there?" I jabbed a trembling thumb toward the four people across the room.

He mashed his lips together and grunted. "That's the house band—what's left of 'em. They lost their horn player last night. Dumbass did some snort, then got roarin' drunk and decided it'd be real smart if he tried crossin' Colonial." He shook his head. "Idiot got himself splattered when he stepped out in traffic. Imagine that? Tryin' to cross Colonial Drive when ya just had a couple snorts and prob'ly at least six shots of rum? Colonial Drive? Gimme a break!"

I sat in frozen silence as the barman whisked away to tend to someone else. Somehow, listening to someone else talk about this made it even worse. It brought the horror closer, making it much more vivid, and a fresh batch of disgust and nausea filled my gut. I downed the rest of my drink. It didn't help.

97

The barman came back. "Want another drink?"

I nodded.

He moved away and came back with the bottle. As he poured, I said, "You sound like you didn't like him very much."

He put the bottle down. "Glen had a good thing goin' here. He was a damn good player—know what I mean? Bastard could play better than anyone I ever heard. That says a lot, since you can count on one hand the number of dynamite bands giggin' nowadays. Most places hire those rapper morons and that loud screamin' shit that'll fry your eardrums in five seconds. The older, more sophisticated crowds don't wanna hear that shit. They like dinner music or jazz that'll help 'em unwind after a rough day at the office. Bits of Jazz had a solid gig here as well as Vizzutti's on Colonial—that's where he was comin' from when he got slammed. They were booked two nights a week here and two nights there, plus they did Disney Village once or twice a week. They'd pack 'em in, too—the older crowd would come here in droves just to hear 'em play. Bits of Jazz specialized in what they called Torch Songs in the day. You know, "*Cry Me A River*?" "*My Funny Valentine*?" That sorta stuff. The group would get everyone all lathered up on the dance floor. Then, after their set, everyone would stagger back to their tables and order more drinks." He frowned. "Bastard threw it all away, that coke habit of his gettin' in the way, along with the booze. They said he was havin' problems with his chick. That explains a lot, but it sure as hell don't justify a prime horn player like him or anyone else cashin' it all in."

"His girlfriend, you say?"

He screwed the cap back on the bottle. Then he jerked his big square head. "That skinny brunette babe sittin' over there with the band. Izzy, everyone calls 'er. She's the one messed him up, although I can't really buy that. The few times I talked to her, she seemed a really sweet, soft-spoken kid. I just think Glen couldn't handle his booze. That boy was as stubborn as they came. A real shame. They had it good here. Now?" He shrugged. "I gave 'em one week to find another good horn player. Otherwise, I gotta cut 'em loose and try findin' another decent band. Wish me luck." He was shaking his head as he stomped back to the shelf to replace the bottle.

I closed my eyes and tried once again to keep the disgust from taking over.

It wasn't your fault.

Somehow it didn't matter. I also kept reminding myself of some of the things the barman just told me—Danny Glen's coke habit...the booze...problems with his girl. That didn't work, either. Guilt was quite possibly the most formidable emotion I could think of. You could justify it—why, when and how you got it—but the end result remained the same. It was strong enough to kill—or at least drive a guy stark-raving mad. I knew damned well that it would kill me if things didn't soon change.

I stared at my drink and decided to drive home after I finished it. After two of these—plus what I'd

99

had back at the condo with Vera—I was already feeling the effects. Normally I could down four or five before deciding to sleep it off so I wouldn't risk my life or anyone else's by getting behind the wheel. But tonight was different. Tonight, I felt much weaker and more vulnerable than ever.

I turned back to face the stage area. Once again, the harsh stabbing of guilt, this time for the surviving members of the band, hit me hard. In one single instant, I not only killed a human being, I'd destroyed a popular local jazz band. The shame descending upon me made it difficult to breathe.

Don't sweat it, dude...

There it was again—that same strange voice. In my present state, I could have sworn someone else had slipped into my head.

Izzy'll get over it...

I don't know...

I do.

But she was the man's girlfriend...

She could have any of the others in a New York second if she wanted...

This was ridiculous. I had to find some way of stopping this weirdness from popping up in my head. I realized that the act of running over a man was an unbelievably serious traumatic event, and would undoubtedly cause all sorts of problems for anyone...

But hearing voices?

It had to stop.

For the first time in my life, I considered going to a therapist. It only made sense. I couldn't fix this on my own. The way things were going, this situation would only get worse. I couldn't afford to let it take over. My life…my career…my profession…everything depended on my state of mind. It was painfully obvious that nothing positive would happen as long as I let this guilt hover over me like a vulture salivating over its next meal.

I decided to wait a couple of days. If the voices didn't stop, I'd make an appointment. This was just too much to take. Hearing strange voices, glimpsing wild images and having bizarre, senseless dreams had to stop.

I drained my drink and left a ten-spot for the barman. Then I got up to leave.

But when I blinked just moments later, I found that I was standing less than five feet behind Izzy's chair, gazing at the back of her head.

Chapter 14

"Somethin' on your mind?"

The guy facing the girl was about thirty, with a scraggly reddish-brown beard and long dark-red hair fastened in a thick ponytail. He wore a long-sleeved blue shirt with a tan leather vest and scuffed jeans. His eyes were hidden behind a small pair of wire-rimmed dark glasses. Although he was sitting, I could tell he was very tall. A burning cigarette dangled from the center of his mouth. I could feel his steady gaze as he pushed a thick ribbon of gray smoke out through his lips and tapped the cigarette lightly on the tin ashtray in front of him.

The girl turned in her chair and looked up at me. Even in the dim lighting, I saw that she was very pretty. Her huge dark-brown eyes were red and wet. Two slender dark lines of mascara had stopped just below her sharp cheekbones. She was obviously grief-stricken, and as her eyes searched mine, I wondered if she could tell why I'd come here.

Could she see something on my face that would give her some clue of what was going on inside me? Could she sense something in my eyes?

Could she look into my eyes and see what happened?

I began wondering what was happening to me. Just moments ago, I'd started to leave, but in the blinking of an eye had come over here without even realizing it. I'd walked over to the group I'd just destroyed and stood over them like a disoriented vulture, unable to account for my own actions.

"You lost?" The guy in the middle of the trio was shorter and stockier than his friend. His beard was also much thicker. A red-and-white checked do rag covered his head, but I could see a short, fat black ponytail protruding from the back. He wore a black windbreaker and faded jeans. The windbreaker was open, revealing a lavender dress shirt opened at the neck and unbuttoned down to his navel. Tattoos were faintly visible amongst the thick black hair covering his chest. However, the tattoos weren't what concerned me. The anger in his dark deep-set eyes told me I'd come too close to his territory and should seriously consider leaving.

"I...just came...to offer my condolences." I knew of nothing else I could say. I didn't want to make their grief—or mine—any worse than it already was by telling them I was the man who'd killed their friend. Since I didn't know them, I had no idea what their reaction would be. The second guy appeared angry enough to get physical. So did the first guy. And I couldn't blame them. I had, after all, destroyed their world.

The second guy didn't respond. He merely stared at the drinks on the table.

The first man gave me what might have passed for a quick half-smile. He then sighed and reached for his glass. While he drank, the third guy mumbled something incomprehensible. He was blonde and broad-shouldered, and appeared several years older than his friends—possibly close to forty.

He was thinning on top and wore a loose gray sweatshirt and matching sweatpants. He grabbed his bottle of beer. His gaze stayed on me as he lifted it.

"Did you...know Danny?"

It was the girl—Izzy—talking. As she stared at me, I could feel her pain so distinctly that I wanted to do whatever it took to wipe the tears from her cycs. I wanted to tell her everything would be fine...that Danny's problems were over...and that she was young and very attractive, and would surely find someone else...

But something inside me told me otherwise. I couldn't shake the strong feeling that she'd never be fine again. Some inner sense told me that the love she'd shared with Danny might have been something very few people experience.

I could tell by the grief on Izzy's face that she'd truly loved the man. Her red eyes, her tears, the paleness in her cheeks, the way she slumped in her seat...everything told me of the horrible devastation ripping through her. Everything on this girl's face told me that her world—perhaps even her life—had been destroyed last night.

But I had to be delicate about this. I realized I was thinking of myself, plus the fact that there were three men just a few feet away who might tear me to pieces if I told them what happened...

However, I was more concerned about Izzy and what it would do to her if I told her.

"*Did* you know him?" she repeated, this time in a whisper.

"No." I couldn't make this worse for her. It was true that I'd never met the man, but I couldn't even remotely suggest anything that might make them suspicious. "The bar guy told me what happened."

She nodded but didn't reply.

My guilt instantly came back. The cops probably hadn't given out any information about me, so I was safe in that respect. But somehow I didn't feel safe. In fact, I felt extremely vulnerable. Once again I wondered if any of them could tell what had happened just by staring at me. My guilt had never felt as real as it did at this particular moment—could it possibly be tangible enough to give me away? Could they see it in my eyes? Sense it in my body language? Could they somehow hear the guilt in my voice?

I turned away from their gaze and suddenly realized I was staring at the leather satchel sitting on top of the piano. It had mysteriously drawn my attention, and I immediately discovered that I couldn't pull away from it.

"Is that…his trumpet?"

Izzy nodded and wiped her eyes with a Kleenex.

"Cops let us have it," Stretch said.

"Danny Boy slept with the damn thing," Blondie said, staring at something on the table.

"He loved that horn." Izzy went back to staring into space.

"It's a French Besson," Do Rag said. "He found it at a pawnshop in Miami. Had to have it. Said it was love at first sight."

"Did anyone ever see if…if—"

"If what?" Stretch asked.

"The damage," I said.

"What the fuck for?" Do Rag asked. "Danny's dead. What the fuck's it matter?"

I shrugged. "I just thought…well, maybe—"

"Maybe what?" Blondie asked.

"Lookin' for a cheap horn?" Do Rag asked.

"Not at all." I was beginning to hate myself for walking over here. Once again I wondered what had possessed me to do it in the first place. I knew that if I persisted with this nonsense, I'd surely give myself away.

"Why so interested?" Stretch asked.

I shrugged. "I don't know. I just think…maybe you ought to see how badly it was damaged."

The four of them stared at me in silence. I began feeling more vulnerable by the second, and expected at least one of them to get up, walk over and begin interrogating me more aggressively. Izzy was the only one not displaying any anger. She seemed more curious than anything else.

Stretch said, "Danny was slammed by a stupid fuck goin' too damn fast in a big car. Cops said he died right there on the spot."

Izzy groaned and covered her face with her hands.

"Horn's prob'ly mashed up good," he added. "It landed on the highway. Cops said it musta flew twenty feet."

I forced myself to keep my mouth shut.

"Totally all fucked up," Blondie muttered.

"Maybe…" I wanted to slap myself in the face. Why couldn't I just shut up and leave this place? What in God's name forced me to come over here and talk to these people? They were angry, torn up, disgusted and frustrated, and here I was, antagonizing them every time I opened my big mouth. Whatever I was doing was stupid and made no sense whatsoever. Yet I found that I was totally helpless.

"You got somethin' to say, man?" Stretch got up and stood with his hands crossed over his chest, looking down at me. I was right; he was close to six and a half feet tall, but probably weighed no more than one-sixty after a heavy meal. "Say it or just get the fuck outa here. We ain't in the mood for bullshit right now."

"Bill…" Izzy wiped her nose with her Kleenex. "Be nice. This man…he's just being considerate."

"How the fuck's he bein' considerate?" Blondie asked bluntly. "He's stirrin' up all sorts of nasty shit."

"Nick, just stop—*please*?" She sniffed and dabbed at her eyes.

"What makes him think Danny's horn's not all fucked up?" Do Rag asked.

"Why don'tcha ask him, Chopper?" Stretch (Bill) sat back down and reached for his drink.

"All right…" Blondie (Chopper) glared at me for at least ten uncomfortable seconds before he spoke. "What makes ya think Danny's horn's not all fucked up?"

"I don't know." I had no idea how I knew. I just had a strange feeling

("*the baby's just fine*")

that the horn was still intact. But I knew I couldn't tell them something like that without getting them even more suspicious, so I had to think of some way of coming out of this relatively unscathed. I decided to improvise and see where this went. "The satchel's pretty big. Maybe—"

"It's a *gig bag*, man," Do Rag (Nick) said.

"It could have a lot of extra padding in it to protect the horn when it was dropped."

"It wasn't *dropped*, brainiac," Bill said flatly. "It was *tossed*."

I didn't reply. I knew damned well that everything I said would be taken the wrong way. But each time I tried to turn on my heel and walk away, I felt as if my shoes were glued to the floor tile. Even so, I knew I had to get out before something horrible happened. The way things were going, it wouldn't be long at all before I said something that would really heat them up. "You're right," I said. "It's probably in pieces."

No one said anything, but they continued watching me.

"Well, like I said, my deepest condolences." This time, when I turned on my heel, my feet obeyed my wishes.

"Wait up." Bill went over to the piano, snatched up the gig bag, hurried right over and handed it to me.

Izzy raised her hand to protest. "*Bill!*"

He shot her a quick glare. "This dude wants to be cute. Let's see just how cute he is."

The moment he'd handed me the gig bag, my heart felt as if it had stopped. I held the bag out in front of me as if I was holding a dead baby in my hands. The leather covering was cold and warm at the same time, and for a moment I could have sworn I'd felt vibrations

(*a pulse?*)

coming from within it.

There is *no pulse,* I told myself. *I'm holding an inanimate object in my hands. A musical instrument made of brass and metal. It isn't alive.*

That's all in the way you look at it, that wretched inner voice said.

It's a brass instrument—not a human being.

It was human to Danny...

I had the strangest feeling some bizarre argument was going on in my head and I was merely a casual eavesdropper.

"Open it, man," Bill said.

"I really don't think I should—"

"Just *open* it, dammit."

"I don't think it's my place to—"

"Open the fucking bag." Bill had taken a step closer—which put him about three feet away. I was close to six feet tall, but he was half a head taller, and his anger made his presence even larger and more menacing.

Despite the circumstances, I didn't want him bullying me. I suspected he was a pushover with an attitude and a big mouth.

But even so, I just didn't want to stand here much longer and let him talk to me like—

Open the bag...

I knew right then that I had to. I had to see for myself if my strange instincts were right—if the horn was still in one piece...

But I didn't know if I could even look at the instrument without coming apart and revealing to these people what had happened...

Just do it!

Whatever was urging me on also seemed to be giving me the courage to accomplish this unpleasant task. I could sense all my fears vanishing, one by one.

However, there were more important things to address at the moment. Bill, Chopper, and Nick were glaring at me, and I could tell they hoped I was wrong. They all wanted me to show them how stupid I was for assuming the horn could still be in good condition.

Izzy hadn't moved. She sat in her chair as before, sobbing quietly and blotting her eyes with a fresh Kleenex. Nick and Chopper had come over and flanked Bill, waiting anxiously to see what was going to happen.

Open it...

I knew at that moment that I was going to open the bag. There was no doubt about it. I turned and placed it carefully on the table behind me. With trembling fingers, I grabbed the zipper and pulled it, until the bag split open. Then I raised the heavy leather flap.

The instrument lay in its soft, black velvet bed, gleaming in the semi dark room. It appeared undamaged.

Dead silence penetrated the area for nearly half a minute.

"Well?" Bill said.

"How bad is it, dude?" Chopper asked.

"It looks...just fine." Though I'd already suspected that the horn would be all right, what baffled me most of all was how it had managed to stay in such pristine condition.

"Pick it up." Bill had moved closer.

"Bill," Nick whispered, "Danny didn't like anyone fuckin' around with—"

"Danny's dead, man. Dead!" The big man's broken voice sounded like he was on the brink of coming apart. "He wouldn't fuckin' care!"

"I...kinda think he would," Nick muttered.

"He's dead," Bill repeated, this time in a whisper.

I grabbed it gently—as if it were indeed an infant. It was cold at first, but the moment I touched it, it grew warm in my hands.

Feel the love coming from it?

Yes.

I held it in front of me, gazing at it as if it was some miracle I'd just stumbled across. It felt like a miracle, and the more I thought of it, the more I realized just how unlikely it was that this light, fragile instrument made of brass and metal had survived such a nasty ordeal. The inside of the gig bag was heavily padded, but it still didn't make

111

sense that the horn would have survived without a scratch.

Then, as I pulled myself away from the horror of the accident and concentrated on the instrument itself, I closed my eyes and immediately saw hundreds of images flashing before me like a movie projector gone berserk. All sorts of things, all sorts of people, and bits and pieces of beautiful songs filled my head. Melodies I'd heard from my father's vinyl collection echoed through my mind.

"Let's see it," Bill said softly.

The man's voice jarred me out of my fantasy. I turned and held it out.

"God *damn*..." Bill gawked at the sight.

"Mother*fuck*!" Nick shivered and turned away.

"Far *out*..." Chopper's eyes filled the sockets.

Izzy stepped around Nick and took a step closer to me. When she realized what she was looking at, she broke down and buried her face in her hands.

Chapter 15

My hands trembled as I reopened the bag.

I had no idea what to do once I'd placed the horn back inside and zipped it back up. Should I hand it over to Bill? Leave it on the table and walk away? Neither option seemed appropriate, but since I couldn't make myself invisible—which would have been my first choice—I had to listen to what my gut told me. I knew only that I had to make myself scarce. I hadn't wanted to be involved with these people in the first place.

But I *had* become involved. And in doing so, I'd not only made a complete ass of myself, I'd stirred them up. The only sensible thing right now was to slip the horn back into its bag as quickly as possible, slither away quietly and hope they wouldn't notice.

You can't go now...

The cursed thought made me want to grind my teeth.

I *had* to leave. I had no choice. These people were *grieving*, dammit. They needed their space. I *couldn't* stick around any longer.

However, some strange force inside me was telling me that I was incapable of leaving.

Was this the same unseen power that had brought me here? Was some unknown destiny giving me orders? Making me do things I didn't want to do? Drive where I didn't want to go? Mingle with these people in their darkest hour?

Or was this merely my own uncontrollable sense of guilt interfering with my actions again?

What in heaven's name was happening to me? If my actions weren't the direct result of my guilt, had I reached the point where I'd chosen to let strange voices in my head control me? If so, I was setting myself up for therapy, the rubber room, and a steady regimen of mind-dulling meds.

I had to ignore the cursed voice—or whatever the hell I kept hearing. Although I had considered seeing a doctor, I refused to believe there was anything mentally wrong with me. My conscience was acting on my guilt complex. Nothing else made any sense.

All I had to do was put the horn back into its bag, turn around and walk away. I'd tried that before, but this time I'd make it stick, and nothing in the world would be able to keep me from—

"How'd you know, man?" Bill was standing close to me. I could smell the beer on his breath.

"P-Pardon?"

"The horn. How'd ya know?"

"Know what?"

"The fucking *horn*, dammit. How'd ya know it wasn't all fucked up?" Although his shades prevented me from seeing his eyes, I could sense a slow, flickering burn growing in them. He was heating up again.

"I didn't."

"Sure sounded like ya did." Chopper had come over. The suspicion glowed brightly in his eyes.

"I just…the bag…it—"

114

"It what?" Nick had appeared on Chopper's left side.

"Were you there?" Izzy whispered, stepping between Nick and Bill.

My pulse raced. Icy tingles hopped down my spine. I forced myself not to tremble. "Was I where?"

She stepped closer. I could smell the vanilla in her hair. "Where Danny...where he...where it happened."

"No. Of course not." The lie came out much easier than I thought. I was normally a horrible liar, but in this case found the truth much too terrible to face. I didn't know if it was because I felt so vulnerable and intimidated with the others standing close. Maybe it had more to do with Izzy's delicate, fine-featured face searching mine. Whatever had happened had made the lie come out smoothly—as if I *hadn't* been there.

"Ya sure?" Bill didn't sound convinced.

"Why would I lie about that?"

"Ya seemed awfully convinced Danny's horn wasn't fucked up," Nick said.

"I was being optimistic. I'm an optimistic kind of guy."

They continued staring. After about thirty seconds of tense silence, they turned around and went back to their table.

Swallowing a lump in my throat, I carefully situated the horn in its niche in the gig bag. I couldn't help noticing how warm it felt once again, and I jerked when I thought I felt a pulse coming from it.

Stop it. You're just stressed from averting a potentially dangerous situation.

Hopefully that's all it was. There couldn't possibly have been a pulse coming from the instrument. I was just overwrought, bewildered and unnerved by the situation. I was also confident that once I left, my brain would resume working properly again. Then I'd realize that the pulse I'd felt had been my own, and the warmth of the instrument had come from the heat emanating from my own flesh.

I zipped it up and straightened. Then I realized Izzy was still standing very close.

I tried once again to hide my fears. I gave her a smile and hoped it looked legit. "I guess I'll be leaving, then."

Before I could move away, she grabbed my wrist and held on. She was a slender girl, not much more than a hundred pounds, but her grip felt like a vise. She moved closer and stared up at me. Even in the dim bar lighting, I could see the intensity in her eyes.

"Something...wrong?" I asked uneasily.

She continued staring. Her eyes had locked onto mine. She was obviously searching for something important—something she needed desperately. Something she thought I could give her. As I returned her gaze, I sensed her in my head, checking for things she needed.

She finally whispered, "I want you to tell me who you are."

"I'm Brad Ellis. I just came over to—"

"No." She closed her eyes and sighed. When she opened them again, they locked onto my own. "I want you to tell me who you *really* are."

Once again I fought hard not to tremble. "That's who I am. Brad Ellis."

She continued staring. The grip on my wrist tightened, cutting off my blood flow. "*Please*?"

"Who do you *think* I am?"

"Your eyes...I can see things...feel things..."

I felt my entire body stiffen and turn cold. "What exactly...do you see?"

Her eyes became fierce slits. She didn't reply.

"Izzy?"

"I'm...not sure..."

Her gaze intensified. The pain in my wrist also increased.

"I really need to go." I made a move to pull away, but she held on tightly.

"*Please* tell me..." She continued holding on. My wrist had already gone numb. I made another attempt to pull away. She finally let go but remained standing there, watching me as she backed away. Two steps later, she blinked, releasing her gaze, and went back to sit at the table with her friends.

Chapter 16

The drive home was just as bizarre as the drive to the bar. I couldn't get the image of Izzy's tear-stained eyes out of my mind, nor could I stop thinking about what happened at the bar.

"I want you to tell me who you are...who you really are..."

What exactly had she seen in my eyes? And why did she stare at me as if she'd been able to see my soul?

Maybe she had. For all I knew, she might have seen everything that happened the moment I'd first come into contact with Danny's trumpet. I know that sounds pretty far-fetched, but strange things had been happening to me, and because of them, I wasn't exactly in the position to rule anything out. The one thing that scared me most of all was that if Izzy was as sensitive as she appeared, she might have picked up on something I'd been trying to hide.

If she happened to be one of those rare individuals who could actually feel or see what was going on inside other people's heads, I couldn't go near her again. If I did, she'd eventually discover my innermost thoughts. If she was truly able to see what had happened, things would not go well for me. The others would learn about the accident, and I'd be a dead man. I couldn't depend on my somewhat naïve assessment that musicians weren't normally violent. Even if I was right in this case, this trio could easily turn vicious if they found out I was the one responsible for killing Danny Glen.

I could never go back to Raymond's. I sincerely hoped that the same strange force that had sent me there wouldn't step in to send me there again.

I got home at around one-thirty the next morning. I was exhausted and wanted to go straight to bed, but instead of shuffling down the hall and stripping off my clothes, I plodded into the kitchen and fixed a drink. I normally didn't drink right before bedtime. I decided that the experience at the bar had rattled me more than I realized. One last drink might calm me down and help me sleep.

I took my drink out into the living room and walked over to the stereo. After some deliberation, I opened the cabinet and grabbed an album. It turned out to be Miles Davis' *Sketches of Spain* LP. I slid the record out of its sleeve, dropped it on the turntable, flicked it on and set the volume on low.

I took my drink over to the sofa, sat back and enjoyed the music until my eyelids could no longer stay open.

***

The moment my eyes closed, a vast darkness swallowed me up.

I was walking down a long, endless tunnel. A tiny light showed at the end, and I could hear a trumpet playing a haunting ballad in the distance. Mindful of the uneven ground beneath my feet, I hurried down the tunnel, my steady gaze on the minuscule light at the other end.

Before I realized it, I'd reached the end and discovered that I was standing in the woods. About twenty feet away, two figures were moving around in the tall grass. They were both female and both naked. One woman lay on the ground on her back, her long red hair spread out on the grass. The woman straddling her was very slender. Her long dark-brown hair dangled over her tiny breasts and slid over the large breasts of the woman lying beneath her.

As I drew closer, the dark-haired woman turned and smiled at me but did not stop sliding her hair sensuously over her partner's breasts. When I was about ten feet away, she gestured in my direction. "Come over here, Brad. Join us."

I went over, stopped a couple of feet away and watched as they continued their lustful efforts. Then the brunette turned to me and giggled. Her eyes had lowered to my groin area.

I looked down.

I was naked as well.

"Come closer," she urged. Then she got up and stepped away from the redhead.

I did as she said, and when our eyes met, I saw flickering flames of fire in her huge dark-brown eyes. Her slender arms reached out for me. Her hands joined at the back of my neck, and she pulled me toward her. The flames in her eyes grew, and in the next moment, their gleaming red-hot tongues lashed out at my face.

The heat inside me intensified. At that same moment, I heard the trumpet ballad playing in my head as well. I tried pulling away, but she held me fast. The heat had consumed me, and I could hear her voice in my head: "Bring him back, Brad...bring him back..."

I had no idea what she meant, but when I closed my eyes, our lips met, and I could see Danny Glen in the darkness of my mind, playing the ballad with his trumpet.

Then, in the next moment, her grip disappeared, and so did the beautiful strains of the trumpet solo. I opened my eyes and saw that she had also disappeared. I was no longer standing. I was bent over, straddling the red-headed woman, my hands around her throat as I choked the life out of her. I tried pulling away, but my hands were fused to her flesh. I struggled even harder, using all my willpower to pull my hands away, and after endless agonizing moments, felt my grip weakening. When I was finally able to wrench my hands away from her, I realized what I'd just done.

Vera lay on the ground beneath me, her face white, her tongue swollen, her glazed eyes staring up at me.

"V-Vera?" Her name trickled out of my throat like a final gasp of air. Forcing myself to snap out of it, I tried shaking her—gently at first, then more vigorously.

In spite of my efforts, she wouldn't wake up.

Panic-stricken, I jumped up and backed away. I couldn't stop gawking at her. Finally I covered my eyes with my hands. "This isn't happening! I didn't *do* this! It's just a *dream*...a horrible, horrible *dream*!"

Then I lowered my hands.

Vera had disappeared. The body lying on the ground at my feet was Danny Glen. And the trumpet solo echoing in the darkness was "*Taps*."

Chapter 17

The morning sun peering through the living room blinds woke me.

As the last remnants of sleep drifted away, I realized that I'd spent the night on the sofa. The record jacket and its sleeve sitting on top of the stereo suggested that I'd put a record on the night before. I couldn't remember doing so. I couldn't even remember why an empty glass sat on the end table.

I sat up carefully and rubbed my eyes. Briefly I wondered if I'd had a nightmare, but my head was cloudy, my thoughts muddled. I had some vague recollection of Vera, and Izzy as well. I also recalled music. This I immediately dismissed since I'd obviously fallen asleep listening to the record.

I shuffled into the kitchen and put the coffee on. Then I went down the hall, stepped into the shower and let the warm spray revitalize me. After toweling myself dry, I went back into the bedroom and dressed.

I decided not to shave this morning; I just didn't feel like it. I wanted only coffee and maybe a little breakfast. However, after further consideration, the idea of eating made me nauseous. I decided to pass on breakfast altogether.

A few minutes later, the coffee was ready. I poured a cup, but when I reached for the sugar bowl, I decided to take it black. I never took my coffee black, but this morning I felt like something different and decided against my usual level teaspoonful.

I went over to the fridge and pulled the door open. Then I wondered what I was doing. Hadn't I decided just moment ago that I wasn't hungry? Why was I now considering breakfast? First, black coffee…now this. Where had my legendary decision-making powers gone? Why couldn't I even remember why I'd spent the night on the couch? And why was I standing in front of the open refrigerator like an idiot?

Since I obviously wanted something to eat, I decided on toast. I got the bread out of the freezer, stuck two slices in the microwave for twenty seconds then transferred them to the toaster. I liked my toast light, but this morning, I watched in total amazement as my index finger pushed the button all the way down to the darkest setting.

A few minutes later, the toast came out black. The sight bothered me, but the smell was oddly satisfying. After smearing them with thick slabs of butter, I decided it would be just fine. I put the slices on a small plate and took my breakfast to the kitchen table.

Just as I sat down, my cell buzzed. I got up, grabbed it from the counter and checked the display. *Dammit*. It was Gloria. I didn't want to talk to her this morning. Hell, I didn't want to talk to anyone from the office this morning. But if I didn't answer, I knew she'd keep trying.

"Hello, Gloria."

"Feeling any better this morning?"

"No." I had a swig of coffee; it tasted quite good. I had another sip. Then I wondered how I could tell her to stop calling me. I didn't want to hurt her feelings, but office matters didn't interest me this morning. I had no idea why I felt this way; I only knew that I didn't want to be bothered.

"Have you seen a doctor?"

"No."

A pause. "Brad? Are you all right?"

"Not really."

"What's wrong?"

I didn't reply right off. Gloria was a good friend and didn't deserve the brunt of my disgusting attitude. But right now, I wanted to eat my toast and drink my coffee.

"Nothing's wrong. I just...I need some time alone."

"You don't sound like yourself."

"Who do I sound like?"

"Well, you sound like you're very far away..."

"You mean there's something wrong with the connection?"

"That's not it."

"What is it, then?"

"I don't know. It's just that, well, you don't sound like your normal self."

"I'm going through something right now."

"Is this some sort of midlife crisis middle-aged men face when they get a little too close to forty?"

"Not in this case..." I didn't want to get into a heavy discussion with her about what was really going on.

"You seemed just fine two days ago, when we were leaving the office..."

"A lot of things have happened since then."

"Wanna tell me about it?"

"No." That sounded unduly harsh, but I had no intention of telling anyone what had happened.

"Okay...so what do I tell the directors? They were pretty steamed that you weren't there yesterday afternoon."

I didn't care about the directors. All I knew was that things strangely felt different and looked different the moment I woke up this morning. I began wondering if I'd somehow reinvented myself. To make matters worse, the moment Gloria had called, I'd experienced a heavy sadness that made me wonder if I'd wasted the last ten years of my life.

"They'll get over it," I told Gloria.

"I'm sure they will, Brad, but that doesn't answer my question."

"What *was* the question?" I experienced genuine embarrassment for not paying attention, but I just couldn't help it.

I heard her sigh. "The directors will be expecting to see you this afternoon. Chuck, Ivan, Betty and the others on the Board were able to deflect some of the heat yesterday afternoon, but I can't guarantee that they'll be as lucky today. They want that merger finalized by the end of the month—which leaves us with less than two weeks to prepare for it."

"What can they do? If I don't want to come in—"

"They're the ones with the money, Brad—remember? They're the folks who helped arrange the merger and put it in motion."

I was getting tired of all this business talk. I hadn't been able to eat my toast or drink my coffee in peace and found that it was getting more difficult to conceal my growing anger. That was probably what had been bothering me in the first place. For the last several years, I'd been putting in close to seventy hours a week at the office. I'd suffered two ulcers, a dramatic weight loss, headaches, reflux from drinking twenty cups of coffee a day, and my alcohol consumption had increased remarkably. At this rate, I'd be approaching heart attack territory before long. I honestly didn't want to die before reaching forty.

"Tell them I'm having a health issue, Gloria."

"I thought you told me—"

"I'm trying to keep it under wraps."

"What is it? Fatigue? Exhaustion?"

"Yes." That sounded good. Both fatigue and exhaustion could be faked without unnecessary suspicion. "It's probably the result of too many late-night hours spent at the damned office. It's finally caught up with me."

"All right…we can work with that. Who do you want manning the helm while you're gone? Chuck? Or Ivan?"

"Chuck's been doing just fine. Ivan's also been doing a bang-up job, but Betty's the one who's been keeping things running smoothly with the directors. Chuck and Betty can make all the decisions on a fifty-fifty basis, with Ivan coming in whenever they need a resolution."

"I'll make a note to put Chuck and Betty at the helm, but Chuck won't like this one bit. And Ivan'll *hate* it."

"Then tell them that I authorized you to have Betty take over."

She laughed. "*That* might take some of the steam out of their pipes."

"Chuck and Ivan are still fairly young. I don't believe either of them has been knocked on his ass yet—not seriously, anyway."

"That sounds somewhat harsh, Brad."

"Getting knocked on your ass gives you character."

"You just might get an argument about that from most of the people struggling to get back up."

"That doesn't make me wrong, does it?"

"No. It doesn't."

PART TWO – IZZY

Chapter 18

After breakfast, I had the irresistible urge to drive to the Fashion Square Mall on Colonial. I hadn't originally intended to go anywhere this morning, but as I cleaned out the coffeepot, I decided that I wanted to shop for some new jazz CDs.

Half an hour later, I walked into Electronics World. The store was large and well-lit, with half a dozen men and women in their early twenties wandering around looking bored and uninterested in their blue shirts and white slacks. Endless rows of computers, hard drives, laptops, and widescreens filled nearly half the store space, with aisles upon aisles of DVDs and CDs on shelves and in racks at the far end, near the refrigerators, microwaves, ovens, washers and dryers.

I went over to the CD section, where signs separated the music into categories. Jazz alone took up four long rows. To make things easier, everything had been filed in alphabetical order.

Starting at the beginning, I selected a CD featuring Cat Anderson, then scanned the B section and grabbed something from Chet Baker on the Verve label, and then a Clifford Brown label recorded in the sixties. I found two albums featuring Miles Davis from the seventies, three Don Ellis recordings from the late sixties, two Maynard Ferguson disks from the late fifties, a rare recording featuring a trumpeter named Conrad Gozzo performing lead in an L.A. studio orchestra, one album with Dizzy Gillespie, two Al Hirt shows from the mid-sixties recorded live at his Bourbon Street bar in New Orleans, and two featuring Doc Severinsen and the Tonight Show orchestra. I also found a couple of Ornette Coleman labels, as well as Johnny Coltrane, Count Basie, Duke Ellington, and Herbie Hancock.

I handed over my credit card at the register. The cashier, a tall, slender guy about thirty, gave me a look of surprise. "A jazz buff, eh?"

I nodded. As I watched him scan the CDs, I wondered what I'd just done. Cat Anderson? Clifford Brown? Conrad Gozzo? Were any of these musicians among my father's vinyl collection? I couldn't remember. I believed there was a Dizzy Gillespie album among the assortment, as well as a couple of Al Hirt records. There were also a few super oldies featuring Count Basie and Duke Ellington, and maybe one with Coltrane.

What about Ornette Coleman? Herbie Hancock?

Had I even heard of those two artists before I came into the store?

"I don't think I've ever heard of this dude." The clerk was studying the Ornette Coleman CD—which made this experience even more bizarre. "You a musician?"

"My dad was a jazz buff."

"I'll bet you inherited his collection."

"Yeah."

"These recordings are from the late fifties. My parents weren't even born yet." He rang me up, bagged my purchases and told me to have a nice day.

Confused and a little shaken, I left the store, trying to determine what I'd just done. After a while, I decided it wasn't worth the trouble. I'd bought some good jazz CDs—there was nothing wrong with that, was there? And it certainly didn't warrant my plunging into a mental panic about it.

Besides, it was nearly eleven-thirty, and I was hungry. My hunger pains were no doubt due to the fact that I'd had such a small breakfast. I slipped into Freddie's Steakhouse at the end of the long hall and took a corner table at the far end in the huge L-shaped room, next to the window that peered out into the hall.

The leggy waitress came over and placed a glossy menu on the mat in front of me. I ordered coffee. As soon as she whisked away, I stared at my bag of CDs and wondered once again what was going on. Why was I so interested in jazz at this point in my life? Was it because I'd accidentally killed a jazz musician? Or was it something else?

You're making a weird situation into something spooky...

For all I knew, the artists whose CDs I'd just bought were also part of my father's collection. I had no idea why I'd come to the mall to buy new CDs, but that sort of thing wasn't *totally* out there in

131

la-la land, was it? Maybe I was just interested in learning more about jazz. Or maybe my dreams were taking their toll on me. I needed to go through my father's collection as soon as I got back home. Once I'd found what I was looking for, I could stop wondering if I was going insane.

I put the bag on the seat of the chair on my left and picked up the menu. Then I glanced at the window on my right.

Someone was standing out in the hall, staring at me.

It was Izzy.

My heart jumped. I let go of the menu; it fell backward. Was it truly her? Or were my eyes deceiving me?

My pulse pounded erratically as I rubbed my eyes. This was my imagination—it had to be. She'd been in my thoughts ever since I'd left the bar last night, and I was almost certain I'd dreamed about her when I sacked out on the sofa. This was no doubt my imagination playing tricks with me by making some total stranger look like her. I told myself that when my vision cleared and I turned back to the window, I wouldn't see her again.

My eyes finally cleared. My pulse still thundered as I turned to the window.

She'd gone—just as I'd hoped.

Sighing in relief, I reached for my menu. I cringed in my chair.

She was standing in front of my table, staring at me.

***

132

"I didn't think I'd see *you* this soon…"

Izzy wore a black tee shirt, designer jeans and open-toed white pumps with two-inch heels. The logo for *The Book Nook* was stitched in white letters on the pocket over her tiny left breast. Above the pocket, a small white tag said, simply, *ISABELLA*, in black letters.

I cursed my miserable luck. Of all the thousands of places in Central Florida, she worked here. She'd obviously seen me from the bookstore and followed me here. Judging by how things were going, she'd probably decided to take her lunch break with me. I wouldn't have minded it so much if the circumstances had been different. She was a beautiful girl. Even so, every time I looked at her, I saw Danny Glen lying dead in the middle of the road.

"I was just doing a little shopping…and decided to have some lunch." I didn't know what else to say.

"Are you meeting someone?"

"No…"

"Well, then…aren't you gonna ask me to join you?"

"I'm sorry." I got up. "Please sit."

She pulled out the chair and sat facing me. She immediately dropped her elbows on the table, rested her chin on her tiny fists and began doing that same eye-searching thing she'd done at Raymond's.

I had to find some way of breaking her hold on me. I was convinced this girl might eventually be able to figure out what was going on in my head. It wouldn't take much for her to feel my torment—or at least sense something wasn't quite right. I didn't want her guessing, and I certainly didn't want to give myself away. Since I'd joined them at the bar last night, I suspected that it wouldn't take much guessing on her part to figure it all out.

"So...you work at the bookstore..." That probably made me sound like an idiot, but I didn't know what else I could say.

She nodded.

As my mind gradually cleared, some things jarred loose, working their way out of the fog. I thought about her grief and suddenly wondered why she'd gone back to work so soon. "Aren't you rushing things just a little?"

"Whaddya mean?"

"I'm wondering why you haven't taken any time off."

She sighed. "There are only two of us handling the floor this week, and they really needed me. They did say I can take off a few days next week, when our manager comes back from vacation."

"Will there be a funeral?"

"Danny's parents are having one in Tampa. That's where they've been living. It'll be a small one—a memorial service. Danny...well, he just didn't like funerals. He thought they were phony, but it's up to his parents, so..." She shrugged.

"I assume you'll be going."

She nodded.

"You'll be taking off work for that, right?"

134

She shrugged. "It's really no big deal, since I'm only working from noon till six anyway. Besides, it's a good job. No one reads much anymore, so it's never crowded. No one messes with me, and the people who talk to me are book lovers, like me. I love it because I need my alone time…and also because I'm allowed to read when no one's in the store. For someone like me, it's the perfect job. There's no stress, and it keeps me busy. And when I do their bookkeeping, no one comes in to interrupt me, so I can take all the time I like."

I nodded.

She began staring again, but I sensed she was looking through me. The feeling was extremely disorienting.

"Why did you come here?" I asked. "You're scaring me, the way you're looking at me. I really wish you'd either say something or just tell me—"

"I wanna know who you are." She lowered her arms. "I don't think you told me everything last night."

A rush of iciness rolled down my arms. It took all the strength I could find within myself to keep from coming apart. Luckily, the waitress came back with my coffee—which interrupted the tension for a few moments. She asked if Izzy would be joining me for lunch. Izzy shook her head. The waitress asked if I was ready to order. I realized only then that I'd lost my appetite. "I'll just have the coffee, thanks."

Once the waitress left, Izzy lowered her voice. "I felt something very strange last night, at Raymond's. I felt it when I saw you."

I needed both hands to pick up my coffee cup. *Stay calm, for God's sake. You have to act like nothing's going on. This isn't some supernatural medium sitting there with you. She's just a sensitive young woman trying to deal with the grief of losing her boyfriend. She can't possibly know anything unless you tell her. So don't tell her anything!*

Even so, the feeling of impending doom hovered frighteningly close.

I managed to coax a few drops of hot coffee into my mouth. Then I swallowed and hoped my voice would work. "What exactly...did you feel?"

"Danny. He was there. I could feel him."

I put the cup down very carefully. My hands were shaking, so I immediately lowered them to my lap, out of sight. "Of course you did." I had to downplay this. "You're grieving. You're bound to feel his presence for a while, but that doesn't mean—"

"It was more than just grief."

It took me a few moments to find my voice. "What was it, then?"

"He was there. With us. I could *feel* him. He was there. I felt it right after you walked over and started talking to us."

I was afraid to ask. "When exactly...did you feel him?"

She gazed even deeper at me, those huge dark-brown eyes pulling me into their space. "When you touched his horn...and especially when you opened the bag, pulled it out and picked it up. It was so totally strange. And freaky. I felt...it was almost as if..." She closed her eyes and sighed.

"Please...tell me." I didn't know why I said that. This was an extremely tense situation. I needed to know exactly what she felt.

Her eyes stayed on mine. "It was like...like Danny was right there, with you...and when you touched his horn, he became alive again."

I felt sweat gathering around my neck. I had to hold on. I couldn't fall apart here, in this restaurant, while people were having lunch. And I certainly couldn't fall apart in front of Izzy.

She had to be imagining all this. There was no way any of this had actually happened. Danny was dead. The fact that she'd sensed his presence demonstrated her grief—nothing else. No one could come back from the dead.

"That doesn't sound possible, you know," I told her.

"I know."

"But you think that's what happened?"

"I *know* that's what happened. I felt him. I *felt* him. He was there. He'd come back...somehow."

"Izzy, he's dead..." I hated being so blunt, but she needed to be reminded of the cold reality of life.

She shook her head. "No. He's not. He's still here."

"But the cops must have told you—"

"I don't care *what* the cops said. Danny may have been run over, but he was right there in the bar. I felt him the moment you opened his gig bag. I sensed his presence. He and his horn…they were inseparable." She sighed and closed her eyes. "I feel it…right now." She opened her eyes. "I feel it…in *you*…"

I had to somehow disprove her theory—not only to her, but also to myself. I knew that if I didn't, several unpleasant things would happen. "You actually feel him…*here*?"

"Yes."

"In *me*?"

"Yes. No. I don't know." She rubbed her eyes. "I only know that I felt him when you opened his gig bag, and when you picked up his horn…" She sighed deeply. She'd turned slightly pale. For a moment I thought she might faint. "He'd somehow come back, and he was standing right there beside you when you picked up his horn and held it. I felt his aura. I honestly did."

I didn't know what to say.

"Did you feel him, too?"

"How's that?"

"When you had his horn in your hands…did you feel his presence?"

"I don't…I'm not sure what you mean—"

"Danny always said his horn had its own heartbeat, its own pulse. He also said that whenever he picked it up, it became part of him, and the cold brass immediately turned warm to his touch. And when he pressed the mouthpiece to his lips, he and the horn became one entity."

Its own heartbeat…

Its own pulse…
Warm to his touch…
Part of him…
One entity…

It was becoming increasingly more difficult to keep my composure. The room had become uncomfortably warm. I wanted to loosen my collar but didn't want to give myself away. I picked up my coffee cup and had another swig. But even as I drank, her words continued echoing through my head. *Its own heartbeat…pulse…his touch…part of him…one entity…*

"You know what I mean." She sat forward. "I can see it in your eyes…"

"I really don't know—"

"Tell me, Brad. Tell me you felt it, too."

"Izzy…"

Her eyes narrowed. "You did feel it, didn't you?"

I couldn't possibly tell her what I felt. It would open up a brand-new world of horror. I'd run over the poor guy, for God's sake. As awful as that was, I couldn't tell his grieving girlfriend what I'd done, nor could I tell her that I'd experienced what she'd just described to me the instant I'd opened the gig bag and touched the horn. Confiding in her would be suicide. And even though I felt terrible for what I'd done, I couldn't possibly subject this gentle soul to more torment.

"No," I said. "I didn't feel anything."

She sat back in her chair and seemed to grow smaller. It made me feel even worse, but I had no idea what else I could have said without making a shambles of this.

"I'm really sorry." I truly was.

She sat there another minute or so, looking down at herself. Then she noticed the bag on the chair beside me. "CDs?"

I nodded nervously.

"Danny had quite a collection—mostly Miles Davis, Doc Severinsen, Clifford Brown, Cat Anderson, and a couple of others I can't remember." She smiled at some fond memory. "And, of course, "the Goz," as Danny always called him."

"The *Goz*?" I could barely hear my own voice.

"Conrad Gozzo. He was Danny's idol. In Danny's eyes, The Goz was God of the trumpet."

Conrad Gozzo. The man was featured in one of the CDs in my bag and recorded by someone I'd never heard of before. It was all I could do to keep from grabbing it, ripping it open and hunting through the stack.

Don't look at it… Whatever you do, don't look at it…

If you bring attention to it--

I sincerely hoped Izzy wouldn't want to see what I'd bought. If she saw some of the labels, she'd freak out.

I struggled to maintain my composure…to think of some sensible reaction to whatever she said or did next…

And, of course, to invent some subtle way of preventing her from checking out my purchases.

She'd gone silent again. After a few moments she snapped out of her memories. "What do you like?" She was looking at my bag of purchases again.

"Like?"

She shrugged. "What did you buy?"

I swallowed and tried my best to keep my brain from freezing up. "I like Foreigner and Journey—that kind of stuff. Moody Blues, the Eagles..."

Please *don't ask to see what I bought...*

She smiled. "I like them, too. I even like the Beatles and the Stones, but Danny was always so busy practicing and listening to his jazz collection, I never had time to listen to my own favorite stuff." She shrugged.

I decided against telling her she could listen to anything she liked from now on. I simply said, "I understand."

She got up and gave me a weak smile. "I'm sorry I bothered you."

I said, "You didn't bother me."

But she'd already turned and walked away.

My nerves continued shaking until she was out of sight. I stared at my coffee and realized it had grown cold. I left a five-dollar tip and got up rather shakily. Before turning away, I stared at my bag, debating whether I should take it with me or just leave it.

Don't be an idiot. There are some tremendous artists in that collection. You're hurting only yourself if you leave them here.

It took me only a moment to decide.

141

I grabbed the bag and left.

Chapter 19

"I'm sorry I bothered you..."

Her words haunted me during my drive back to Winter Park. It made me feel even worse. To clear my head, I flicked on the radio and listened to several commercials, the weather forecast and a Beatles song from the mid-sixties.

But it didn't work. Her words wouldn't stop ringing in my ears.

I didn't know if the phrase bothered me because of the guilt I was already suffering or because she was actually right. I'd told her she hadn't bothered me at all, but as I gave it more thought, I realized she had. She was a beautiful girl with an inner softness I'd never seen before...but each time I saw her, I felt like a monster and wanted to kill myself.

It's your guilt. She's making it worse every time you see her.

Once I got back home, I put the bag of CDs on top of the stereo cabinet, got a drink from the kitchen and went back into the living room. My cell buzzed, but I ignored it. I didn't even check to see who it was. I didn't care. I had other things on my mind.

I spent the next half-hour sitting on the sofa, sipping my drink, thinking about Izzy and staring at the bag while gathering the courage to open the cabinet. I had no idea what I'd do if the artists in question weren't among my father's collection. If

143

this were the case, I'd spend the rest of the day wondering how I even knew about these guys.

You're gonna drive yourself crazy…

I already knew that. I also knew that it wouldn't be a very long drive. After all, I'd just spent three hundred bucks on a batch of CDs recorded by artists I'd never heard of before. Who in his right mind would do something like that?

I finished my drink, got up, took two steps toward the stereo, and stopped cold. My pulse raced and I found that I couldn't even look at the cabinet. I obviously needed another drink.

I went back to the kitchen, filled the glass again and came right back. Then I collapsed on the sofa and spent the next fifteen minutes trying to gather my courage again.

I was being ridiculous. I was using Scotch to give me the courage to check out a batch of old records. I was a grown man, for God's sake, and if I didn't have the stones to do check out a bunch of old record covers, I had no business sharing the planet with other people obviously much more capable than I was of handling infinitely more complicated problems than that.

Angry with myself, I got up, went over and opened the cabinet. Then I sat down on the carpet and forced myself to the task at hand.

It didn't take much time at all to pull the records out of the cabinet, check each one and push them right back. There were about a hundred and fifty in total. It took no more than a second or two to glance at the names of the artists and their bands displayed boldly on the covers.

It took me about ten minutes to check them all, and by the time I'd finished, I realized that the hair on the back of my neck had bristled.

"Danny had quite a collection--mostly Miles Davis, Doc Severinsen, Clifford Brown, Cat Anderson, and a couple of others I can't remember. And, of course, "the Goz," as Danny always called him."

There were no Cat Anderson LPs in Dad's collection. There was also nothing by Clifford Brown or Chet Baker. To make matters worse, I saw nothing by Ornette Coleman, Conrad Gozzo, or Herbie Hancock.

So how did I even know about them?

And what made me pick out their recordings at the store?

***

I sat on the sofa, gazing at the stack of new CDs on the cocktail table as if they were an intruder that had snuck into my home.

As hard as I struggled to analyze this, I found that I had no idea why I'd purchased them or why I'd even gone to the store in the first place. It made no sense. None of this did.

After a while, I realized it didn't matter. I was obviously making entirely too much out of it. If I looked at this objectively, I'd see that none of this should concern me at all.

Since I'd always loved music and admired anyone capable of playing a musical instrument, my guilt for accidentally killing a musician had made me much more sensitive to what I'd done. My father had been a jazz buff for most of his life. I fondly remembered him sitting in his recliner in the living room after dinner, listening to his favorite artists. I didn't remember the artists or the music, but I had played several the albums during the last few years and had been pleasantly surprised that the music remained just as addicting now as it had been decades earlier.

You need to listen to them. Just sit back and enjoy...and forget about everything else.

Without hesitation, I opened up the first one I found in the bag, which turned out to be Cat Anderson. I slipped it into the player in the console cabinet. Then I returned to the sofa, sat back, and closed my eyes.

The music was incredible. I began to relax, until the trumpet and the strings faded into the darkness.

Izzy's face appeared in the darkness. Her eyes were enormous. "Who are you? Who are you really?"

"I told you who I am."

"I don't think you know who you really are."

"I've already told you. I'm Brad Ellis."

She blinked, and a tear slid down her cheek. "I feel Danny with me all the time. I feel his presence even stronger when I'm with you."

I didn't respond.

"He's with you, Brad. I can feel him."

"You're wrong."

146

"Why is he with you?"

"He's not. He's dead."

Her face moved closer. "Danny's not dead."

"Yes he is."

"How do you know for sure?"

I didn't reply.

"Please tell me…"

"I can't."

"Please *tell me!*"

I swallowed a lump in my throat.

"Brad? Please?"

"I…I saw him die."

She blinked again. More tears rolled down her cheeks. "How did…how did you…see him die?"

I couldn't speak.

"How?" Her eyes reddened. Flames flickered in them. "How did you see him die?" The flames grew, reaching out for me. "Tell me, Brad! *Tell me!*"

The flames lashed out. Tongues of fire encircled me. I gasped and cried out. The flames gradually died. Izzy disappeared. The darkness evaporated and turned into my living room again. I realized only then that the music had stopped.

I'd had another strange dream. But I could still hear Izzy's words floating around in my head. *"He's with you… I can feel him…"*

I immediately began cursing myself for our last encounter.

How could I have lied to her like that? The poor girl was destroyed. And it was no wonder. I'd taken the love of her life away from her forever. I'd

147

torn her life apart and, in a split second of carelessness, darkened her future. Whatever would possess me to turn away from her? Why had I treated her as if she was some disgusting psycho who'd been stalking me?

She *wasn't* some disgusting psycho. She was a beautiful, sensitive young woman. Danny Glen's death had been haunting me so much that my entire life had been turned upside-down.

However, this wasn't all about me. Izzy was affected by this infinitely more than I was. Also, the members of his band—as well as his friends and family—were coping with the tragedy. And when I saw those grief-stricken eyes in the tear-stained face of the young woman who'd loved him and shared her life with him, I wanted to curse myself for how I'd treated her in the restaurant.

I am a monster. I really and truly am...

Izzy needed to know what happened. She had to know that I was the one who'd killed her boyfriend. But she also had to know the circumstances. She needed to be told Danny hadn't made any attempt to move out of the way. She had to know that he was watching me in a strange, morbid fascination the moment I'd hit him.

I couldn't go on like this any longer. I had to tell Izzy what happened.

Chapter 20

My heart pounded wildly as I parked the BMW in the front lot of Fashion Square Mall at around four o'clock.

For the next twenty minutes, I sat behind the wheel and struggled to keep my nerves under control while considering what my next move would be. Should I just walk inside as planned, then march into the bookstore and tell her what happened? Or should I do the sensible thing and drive back to the condo?

Sensible? Or Cowardly? Either decision would no doubt lead to a very unpleasant end. What could I accomplish by walking into the bookstore and telling Izzy that I was the man responsible for killing Danny Glen? Did I think this would make things better? Was I under the delusion that this would provide her closure? Could I assume that she'd be able to sleep better when she finally discovered what happened? That everything would turn out just fine and dandy once she'd seen the face of the man who'd accidentally took her boyfriend away from her forever?

No matter what it would or would not accomplish, I didn't think I had much of a choice. Izzy suspected something was going on with me—something that involved her dead boyfriend. I didn't think I could just let this go. I truly believed I had to set her mind at rest and tell her what I'd done. It wouldn't be easy for either of us, but I didn't think I could just walk away without at least trying to resolve this.

I got out of the car, trudged up the aisle and stood in front of the glass doors, staring at my pitiful reflection while trying my best not to loathe myself for bringing about all this depression and heartbreak to so many people. After several more minutes of fruitless deliberation, I took a deep breath and gathered up the courage I needed to walk inside.

A couple of minutes later, I reached the wide archway of the Book Nook. Less than twenty feet from where I stood, Izzy was pushing a cartful of hardbacks over to one of the displays.

Only then did I realize just how difficult this was going to be. I stood frozen at the entrance, my palms sweating while I struggled with the torment that had already consumed me. I tried very hard to convince myself that the smartest thing I could do was to turn around and walk back to the car. But as I watched her, my heart softened again, and I couldn't bear the burden of knowing that I'd caused this beautiful quiet soul so much grief and had done nothing to help her through this.

Just then, she straightened, turned, and stared directly at me.

I cursed myself again. I should have turned around and left when I'd first considered it. Now I had no choice but enter the bookstore.

She met me halfway, those enormous orbs latching onto my own. "Why are you here?" she whispered.

It was a simple question, one that required a simple answer. Yet I couldn't find the right words.

"Did you wanna buy a book?"

"No..."

"Then why are you here?"

It took me a moment to get my thoughts together. The instant she'd begun staring at me, my mind had gone blank, and I had to struggle to remember why I'd come here. Once the reason came staggering back, I knew right then that I couldn't say anything that would fill those beautiful eyes with tears. "I...really don't know."

She continued gazing at me in silence. She finally took another step toward me. Her eyes stayed on me, pulling me in, just as she'd done so many times before. I could tell she was doing her thing and doing it quite well. I could feel her sensing my vibes. Once again, I suspected she'd gone inside my head. "Are you *stalking* me?" she asked finally.

"*No*." I hadn't thought she'd consider something like that. "I'm not a stalker."

"Then tell me why you're here."

"This was a bad idea. I'm sorry I interrupted you in your work." I turned to leave.

"You know, don't you?"

I turned around. She'd moved closer and stood just a couple of feet away, her expression a mix of anger and confusion.

"Pardon me?"

"You know what happened. I know you do."

"I *what*?" I could barely hear my own words. I could tell by her expression and by her words that I'd been right all along. She had indeed peeked inside my head. She might not know exactly what was in there, but I was certain she had some idea.

"You know what happened…with Danny. I know you do."

I couldn't feel the floor beneath my feet. I began having trouble breathing. I wanted to loosen my collar but was unable to lift my arms. They weighed a ton.

"You know. I can tell. I can see it…in your eyes…"

I swallowed and was eventually able to speak. "He was run over…I heard that—"

"You know more than that, don't you?"

I wanted to reply, to tell her what I'd planned to tell her before, but something inside me resisted. I strongly felt that I'd collapse if I said anything else. Her gaze held me fast. I could have sworn I saw something in her eyes—a shadow? a flicker of darkness?—and realized at that moment that I was powerless to say anything.

"*Please* tell me what happened…how you know…what you saw…"

"I really need to go."

"You're troubled, Brad. I can feel it."

Chills suddenly overwhelmed me. This girl was doing something to me that I couldn't describe or even understand. I had to get away from her. I had to get away, period. I'd found it very difficult to breathe.

"*Please* tell me…"

I took a deep breath and concentrated on getting my voice—as well as my thoughts—back under control. The chills remained there but were manageable. "I'm sorry I came here…I really need to leave."

"If you know, you have to tell me!"

"I *don't know*!"

"*Please*?"

I hurried back out and practically ran down the hall, past small throngs and staggered clots of shoppers. When I reached the end of the long hall, I stopped and turned around.

Izzy was standing out in the middle of the hall, watching me. She was perhaps two hundred feet away, but I could tell she was watching me, and I could have sworn I heard her soft voice in my head saying, "*Please* tell me what happened to Danny…"

***

A cold numbness enveloped me as I sat on a stool in the coffee shop, gazing at the busy mall parking lot across the street.

I fought hard to keep the panic at bay while struggling to determine what I had to do to cleanse my soul of this nasty business. I could feel my existence growing darker by the hour, telling me I had to do something. I had no idea what I *could* do; I only knew that if I didn't do *some*thing, I'd lose myself.

My cell buzzed. I checked the display. It said *Gloria*.

It took me a moment to remember who Gloria was. When it finally registered, a sliver of fear sliced down my spine. I'd known Gloria for years—what the hell was happening to me?

"Hi, Gloria."

"Brad, we're beginning to have trouble with the merger."

Merger. Merger. Once again, my brain seemed to have taken a short vacation while I wasn't looking. It took me several moments to realize what she was talking about. I forced myself to forget about my present dilemma and concentrate…and after just a few tense moments, more of my brain cells finally began firing up. In no time, I felt like my old self again.

I really needed to start paying attention. This was my business, wasn't it? My career. My livelihood. The main reason I was able to pay off that condo. This merger was the result of something I'd been working on for some time.

So why did it suddenly feel unimportant? Why did I no longer seem to care?

"Tell me what's going on." I tried to sound concerned but wasn't sure it came out that way. The moment I'd said it, I realized that I wasn't really concerned at all. For some reason, I found that I was more interested in what was going on at the Book Nook at the Mall—which was why I hadn't taken my eyes from the front, where Izzy would eventually come out to get in her car.

While Gloria went into excruciating detail about the problems they were having with two of the directors, I found myself zoning out. Instead of listening, I thought about Izzy and what I had to do about this. I thought about the first time I saw her at Raymond's, sitting at the table, dabbing at her eyes with Kleenex. I saw her standing off to the side, gazing at me as I opened Danny Glen's gig bag...and when I took Danny's horn in my hands...and when she gripped my arm as I tried to leave, her eyes burning into my soul. And then at the Book Nook. And at the restaurant.

And then, finally, out in the hall. "Please *tell me what happened to Danny...*"

I can't do this anymore!

I told Gloria I'd think about what she told me. I also told her I'd have an answer for her soon. However, I could tell by her silence—as well as the chill in her voice when she'd agreed to my terms—that she didn't appreciate my response.

I pocketed the cell and immediately focused on my present dilemma. I knew I'd made a big mistake by letting Izzy see me. I also knew what could happen if I told her I was the one who'd accidentally killed Danny.

Nothing good could possibly come out of this.

But in spite of all this deliberation, I didn't see any other way of handling this. I didn't know if I was looking for closure for myself or for Izzy. What I did know was that I could never be the person I once was. I'd killed a human being—how could I possibly think anything would ever put my spirit back together?

I finally realized that it would probably be best if I didn't do anything at all. What exactly would a confession accomplish? Would it make her feel better? Would it make her whole again? Would it make *me* whole again?

I was torn between doing the right thing and doing the sensible thing. Each time I looked into Izzy's eyes, I loathed myself. Her tears. The intense sadness on her face. The shadow veiling her eyes. The tremor in her voice. Everything slammed mercilessly through me.

She definitely knew something was off. I had no idea if she was just guessing or if she genuinely had some unique gift. Whatever it was horrified me and told me how little it would take for her to figure it all out if I gave her half a chance.

I couldn't give her that chance. No matter how badly I felt, I had to step away and make myself invisible. Despite my good intentions, I had to accept the obvious fact that Izzy and I would be much better off keeping our distance from one another. I also had to convince myself that I needed to get back to my former life and resume living it.

And, of course, try very hard to put this behind me.

I finished my coffee and drove back to Winter Park. I caught myself glancing in the rearview more than a dozen times during the short trip home. After a while, I told myself how stupid I was acting. I needed to focus on the road ahead.

I also needed to try really hard to forget about what I'd left behind…

Chapter 21

I got home just twenty minutes later.

To take my mind off my frustrations, I decided to put on one of my new Clifford Brown CDs. While it played, I fixed myself a rum and Coke. I hadn't had rum in years. For some reason, I wasn't in the mood for Scotch. Just as Clifford went into his version of "*Yesterdays*," I took the bottle and my glass into the living room, plopped down on the sofa, and closed my eyes.

Just a couple of minutes later, the doorbell buzzed.

Cursing at the intrusion, I lay back and closed my eyes again. There was really no need to answer the door. I wasn't in the mood for visitors or conversation. I wanted to listen to the soothing music so I could concentrate on something other than hating myself. I couldn't do that very well if I had visitors, could I?

The doorbell buzzed again.

Dammit!

Groaning, I got up, crossed the room, and stomped over to the front door. Without bothering to glance at the peephole, I yanked the door open.

Izzy was standing on the front porch.

An icy chill sliced through me. My limbs went numb, and I discovered I was unable to move. My world had suddenly become terrifying again. I opened my mouth, but nothing came out. Since I had no idea what I could have said right then, I was somewhat relieved.

But it was no wonder. I soon found that I could barely breathe. My mind had gone berserk, my thoughts spinning around like a carousel gone wild. The only thing I could comprehend was that Izzy was standing on my front stoop, gazing at me with those haunting brown eyes.

"Can I…come in?" she asked in a soft voice.

I took a deep breath and tried to collect myself. It took me three tries to get the words out. My mouth felt as if it had been stuffed with cotton. "How did you know…I live here?"

"I honestly don't know."

"Then…how did you know to—"

She shrugged. "Can I come in?"

I took another breath. It helped, but that same frozen state of numbness continued to grip me tightly. What she'd just said made no sense at all. "Were you following me?"

She shook her head.

It was difficult to believe she hadn't followed me. My first thought was that she might have looked me up in Google. Finding someone in an area the size of Central Florida would take considerable time and research. Yet I'd only known her a few hours. And she'd spent most of her day working at the bookstore. "You just came here? Without knowing where I live?"

"I think I was brought here…"

A lump gathered in my throat. "Brought here? By whom?"

She went silent and looked down at her feet. A few moments later, she met my gaze. "I think it was Danny…"

Another avalanche of chilling ice swept through me. Danny had brought her here. Danny was dead, but he'd somehow brought her here.

"Can I *please* come in?"

I didn't know what else to say. The girl had found her way here; I couldn't turn her away. I'd already turned away from her at the mall and loathed myself for doing so. But even so, I found that I didn't want her here on my doorstep. I wanted her to go away. Being this close to her and looking at her sorrowful face consumed me with so much guilt that I couldn't stand myself. I just didn't know how I could send her away without hating myself for the rest of my life.

I gestured for her to come in.

Her head still lowered, she slipped by me.

I closed the door. My hands trembled, and my legs shook at the knees. The moment the door latched shut, more iciness swept through me. I felt that I'd let some disgusting strain of evil into my home—that my deepest fears would now be trapped in my modest sanctuary.

I stood stock-still in frozen terror, trying to get my trembling under control as I stared numbly at the door. Part of me wanted to believe that I'd only imagined Izzy coming to my home. After all, there was no logical reason for her to be here in the first place. She had no idea where I lived. It would take someone several days to find someone without using Google or the phone book. All I had to do was turn around to make sure. I'd quickly discover that I was alone. Then I could return to the sofa and continue listening to Clifford Brown.

After a few deep breaths, I turned around.

She was standing there, watching me. "Can I sit down?"

It *wasn't* my imagination after all.

"Brad? Is it all right if—"

"Yes. Please sit. I'm sorry. Would you...like a drink?"

She went silent for a few moments. Then she turned her head toward the stereo. "You're listening to Clifford Brown." Her voice was a whisper.

"Yes."

She took in a deep breath. I knew what she was thinking.

"A lot of people like Clifford Brown," I said.

She nodded but said nothing.

"He's popular with jazz buffs."

Another nod.

"Please sit."

She went over to the sofa and glanced at my half-filled glass. Then she stared at the bottle. Her face paled, and she froze. "Is that...wh-what...you're having?"

"It's rum and Coke."

She trembled.

"Izzy? What's wrong?"

She swallowed. "That was...Danny's drink..."

***

160

Her simple statement worsened my present state of numbness.

My brain went totally blank as I desperately struggled for an explanation. I finally settled on something vague and innocent—something that wouldn't prompt her to read anything else into it. "I usually drink Scotch. Tonight I thought I'd have something different…"

"But why rum?" She didn't take her eyes off the bottle.

"I don't know. It was the first bottle I grabbed." I had to get her mind on something else. "What would you like?"

"I don't like alcohol very much. It upsets my stomach."

"You can't drink at all?"

"Almost never, but when I do, it's usually rum and Coke."

I should've known. "How do you like it?"

"I have to have it very weak. Just a tiny splash of rum would be enough."

"With ice?"

"Please."

I grabbed a glass in the kitchen, dropped two cubes in it, poured enough Coke to half-fill the glass and came right back. I picked up the bottle, poured about a quarter of a shot into the glass and handed it to her. She smiled briefly, avoiding my eyes, and took a tiny sip. Then she put the glass in her lap and stared at it.

"Please tell me how you found me." I sat down beside her. "I can't believe you just came here—especially since you didn't even know where I live."

"As I said before, I'm pretty sure I was brought here…"

Once again, I didn't know what to say. Her statement would have sounded ridiculous if I hadn't experienced the same thing when I'd driven to Raymond's on the Trail instead of stopping at a lounge closer to home on Semoran, as I'd originally planned. Nothing had happened in a logical way since the night I'd killed Danny Glen. I just didn't know why. It had to be more than my guilt stirring things up, but I had no idea how else I could explain any of this.

"You don't believe me…" She'd been watching me closely.

It took me a while before I could reply. I couldn't tell her what had really happened, so I had to find some way to convince her I didn't think she was a fruitcake. "Actually, I think I understand."

"Really?"

"I think so…"

"Then I wish you'd tell me, because I don't."

"I thought you said you could sense things."

"That doesn't explain why I'm here."

"You obviously came to see me."

"I honestly believe Danny wanted me to come here."

"Why?"

"I keep getting these vibes. They're telling me I need to talk to you…that Danny could be trying to communicate through you."

I wanted so much to believe this was merely her imagination. Just because she'd said this didn't necessarily mean it was happening, did it? Yet I couldn't help thinking that she might be right about the whole thing. "Any idea why?" I asked.

"I was hoping you might be able to tell me."

This was getting even more frightening.

Just then, she looked me right in the eye. "I can't get over this feeling…that you somehow know…that you've got something to do with Danny…"

I picked up my glass with trembling hands and drained it. "I never met the man."

"Then why would he bring me here? Why do we keep coming together?"

I put down my glass rather unsteadily and gazed at it so I wouldn't have to look at Izzy. I could tell that she was so close to figuring this all out right now that anything she saw on my face would tell her the full story. I had to get her off the subject. "Tell me about when the two of you met."

She smiled. Her eyes lit up, and all the lines on her face disappeared. For the very first time since we met, she seemed to come alive.

"We practically grew up together. We lived next door when we were kids and had a crush on one another in high school. We went together in our senior year, in downtown Erie."

"Pennsylvania?"

163

She nodded. "Danny was in the band, of course, and I was in the book club and chess club and all those other brainy things. Then Danny's father was transferred to Florida, and his family moved to Orlando. It happened in the summer, right after we'd both graduated." She lowered her head. When she looked at me again, it was as if all the light had gone out of her eyes. "It was the saddest summer of my life. My world had fallen apart."

"So how did you get back together?"

She began smiling again. "That was the most miraculous thing about all this. Before Danny and his family moved away, he came to see me. He told me he'd find some way for us to get back together, and once that happened, no one would ever split us up.

"Three years went by. I'd gone to the local branch, majoring in English Lit and minoring in Accounting, and worked at the local supermarket, doing their bookkeeping until I got my degree. I'd saved up all the money I'd made at the supermarket and decided to use it to move to Florida and find him. I knew he was still in Orlando—we'd been calling one another, texting and sending cards all this time—so I knew where to start looking. He'd moved out on his own about a year after they moved to Orlando. His father was transferred again, this time to Tampa, but Danny wanted to stay in Orlando because it was much easier getting gigs. He'd been playing with a couple of bands and was moving around a lot. He'd given me an address, but since he was always on the road, I knew it might not be easy finding him."

"Did you call and tell him you were coming down?"

She shook her head. "I wanted to surprise him."

"Orlando's a big place."

"That didn't matter at all. I found him the second day I came here. I booked a room at a motel not far from his last address, rented a car and began looking for the night spots. I was already twenty-one, but since I'd never liked drinking or partying, I didn't know anything about nightclubs. But it turned out that I didn't have to know. The second day I was here, I stopped at one of the 7-Elevens in the area, and as soon as I got out of the rental to pump some gas, I heard a trumpet playing. I thought it was in my head at first, but it seemed to be everywhere, and I could tell it was Danny. I finished up at the pump, and when I got back in the rental, I had this strong feeling that I knew where he was. I drove a mile or so and parked along the curb in a subdivision on Rio Grande. I still heard the music, so I knew I was close. My heart was practically in my mouth when I jumped out of the car and ran up the driveway, and the moment the music stopped, I knocked on the garage door." Her face beamed. "The door raised open, and he was standing there, holding his trumpet. He'd been rehearsing with his band."

"And you heard him all the way from the 7-Eleven?"

165

"Strange, isn't it?" She was still smiling. Her eyes glistened.

"That's beyond strange."

"From that day on, we were always together. We even made a pact that we'd stay together—even after death."

"What?" I didn't think I'd heard her right.

"I'd been studying spirituality and all sorts of religions since I was a little girl and discovered long ago that death is merely a different room in a different plane, and when two souls bond and remain very close, they become one entity and never really separate. We promised one another that when the time came, whoever passed first would find some way to communicate with the other."

"Are you a medium?"

"No."

"A psychic?"

"Not really—although most people I know have always thought I was."

"What's the difference?"

"A psychic tunes into a person's energy by feeling or sensing elements of their past, present, and future. Mediums—well, they go a step further and actually communicate with spirits who've passed."

"And you're neither?"

"My feelings deal with intuition and sensing vibes from other people. I'm actually just an empath."

"What's that?"

She shrugged. "I'm just one of those people who happen to be overly sensitive. I've always been that way."

"Overly sensitive?"

"Very."

"You mean you can actually sense things?"

"I can sense, feel and see things most others can't."

I began growing uncomfortable again.

"Most people find me very strange," she said. "I tend to make them uncomfortable."

I knew exactly what she was talking about.

"You know what I'm talking about, don't you?" she asked.

I shifted in my seat. "How did you know what I was—"

"As I just said, I can tell."

"Don't be frightened of me, Brad. Please? It's not like I can sense *everything* about you, you know…"

"I guess it all depends on what you can actually sense…"

"Empaths are usually super-sensitive about things others don't even notice, or just take for granted. I sense other people's feelings, especially when they're strong emotions."

"How about body language?"

"I'm really good at that."

I didn't reply, for obvious reasons.

She sighed tiredly. "Being an empath has its disabilities, believe me. For one thing, I can't tolerate much negativity. It puts me into severe depression. Crowded spaces frighten me as well as loud noises, and I can't handle pain very well."

"And you don't drink much."

"I'm extremely sensitive to meds and stimulants."

"Are there any benefits to this...condition?"

"I wouldn't call it an actual *condition*..."

"I...didn't mean it like that." I hoped I hadn't hurt her feelings.

"It's all right," she said, and I could tell she'd sensed my discomfort. She smiled. "But there are benefits, believe it or not. I'm very conscientious. People are always telling me I'm a great listener, so they come to me whenever they have problems, or just when they need to talk to someone. And since I can't tolerate meds or stimulants, I'll never have to worry about being addicted to drugs or alcohol."

"I guess that's something..."

"The important thing is that Danny and I...well, we've always been closer than most couples." She looked away. I sensed that she'd suddenly gone back to the past and began remembering something important. When she looked at me again, her eyes were wet. "The horrible thing about all this is that I knew something bad was going to happen the night he...that night."

"How?" I didn't want to know but heard myself asking anyway.

"I don't know. I just knew."

"That intuition thing?"

"Like I said, I'm very sensitive and can sense all sorts of things. Some of them good, others not so

168

good. The bad thing about it is that I can't pick and choose. Everything eventually comes to me, sometimes all at once. That night...well, I just sensed this darkness that kept trying to swallow me up."

"Darkness?"

She nodded. "With me, darkness and doom are the same thing."

"That makes sense."

She began staring at the carpet at her feet. "Anyway, since we were so close, I could tell something awful was going to happen. Ever since the police called and told us about the accident, I've had this strong feeling that he's trying to come back." She gazed at me. "Brad, I can tell he's close. I can really feel it."

I knew better than reply.

Izzy sat forward. Her eyes still glistened. "He's using you, Brad," she said in a soft voice. "For some reason I just can't figure out, Danny has latched onto you."

I didn't know what to say. I was furiously trying to come up with something that would discourage her from pursuing this. My best bet was to convince her that I had no idea what she was talking about. This way, I might be able to steer her away from this before she got even closer. "I don't know about that..."

"I do."

Her eyes were dead-steady. Her expression suggested she was getting closer by the second. But I had to somehow keep myself from losing what composure I kept clinging to. I decided to try and find out exactly what was going on in her mind. Otherwise, I'd have to guess, and I knew how foolish that would be, doing something like that with a woman like her. "But why would he want to use *me*? Why would he pick *me* to help him come back?"

She took a deep breath. "I really don't know why."

"Then what makes you think—"

"I don't know, Brad. All I can say is that every fiber in my being is telling me Danny has chosen you and you alone to bring us back together."

Chapter 22

"Bring us back together..."

I sat in stunned silence. Was it possible Izzy could be right? What she'd just said sounded totally insane. How could a dead man possess the power to choose me or anyone else to bring him back?

Did this explain the strange voices I'd been hearing the last couple of days? Did it explain my bizarre behavior?

Despite all this, I didn't want to accept the terrifying fact that Danny Glen's spirit had been influencing me. I didn't even believe in stuff like this—how could I believe anything Izzy was saying?

"For some reason I just can't figure out, Danny has latched onto you."

Was that really what had happened? Or was this just my imagination working on my guilt again?

As I thought about the last couple of days, I realized that I wasn't sure about anything anymore.

However, as I struggled to validate what might actually be going on, I suddenly realized that the most disturbing thing of all had nothing to do with what Izzy had just said. As I gazed into the woman's eyes, I found that I wanted to devour her.

She's a hot lady...

I didn't need to hear a strange voice in my head stating the obvious. Izzy was indeed an extremely desirable woman.

This made things even more frustrating. I was sitting next to a beautiful woman and knew full well that I couldn't take advantage of her. It was bad enough that I'd taken away the man she'd loved. If I did the unthinkable and had my way with her, I'd never be able to look at myself in the mirror.

"You must think I'm mental," she said, watching me.

She was apparently sensing my confusion. I had no idea how developed her abilities actually were, but I could tell by her expression that she was definitely aware that my brain was in utter turmoil.

"I really don't," I told her.

"Then…you *believe* me?"

"I honestly don't know *what* I believe."

"How else could I have gotten here? How else could I have found you?"

"I wish I had an answer to that."

"Do you have any idea why I keep sensing Danny's presence when I'm with you?"

It took all my inner strength to keep from telling her the obvious. I didn't know how much longer I could go before she guessed what happened the other night.

"You must've been *fairly* close when Danny died," she said. "How else could he have found you? How else could he know about you?"

"I was probably in the area that night…" My throat felt constricted. "After all, my office is in downtown Orlando."

"That area is one of the most highly-populated in Orlando. There are restaurants everywhere, two major malls, theaters, half a dozen strip malls, gas stations at every corner..."

I just shrugged.

"Doesn't it mean anything to you that he picked you over everyone else?"

My pulse hammered. "I honestly don't know if he did. Izzy, this is all speculation. I respect your opinion, but—"

"Then you *do* think I'm crazy..." She suddenly looked very tired.

"It's not that at all."

"What *is* it, then?"

"I'm just not...well, I'm not quite sure about death or the afterlife. I never have been."

She gave me the sort of look one gives to someone who has just said something asinine. "You...don't believe...in the afterlife?"

"No. Yes. Sometimes. Like I said, I'm not sure."

"*I* am..."

"How can you be so sure?"

"I've been reading about this stuff since I was a little girl. I must've read a thousand books on it. It exists, Brad. It truly does."

"I just don't know how anyone can be so sure about something as abstract as that."

Her eyes grew in excitement. "I've seen so much evidence of it...and of God...and of things that don't make any sense but happen anyway."

I shrugged but didn't reply.

"You've got to be receptive, Brad. Not all things can actually be seen to be believed."

"I guess I've been much absorbed with logic and reality all my life to have even considered the alternative."

"It's not too late, you know…"

You know you want her…

That damned voice again. I rubbed my temples and tried once again to block it out but found it much more difficult. I didn't know if it was her smell, her voice, her gentleness…or the delicious closeness of her. Whatever it was, it seemed to be gaining strength. To make matters worse, I could feel my self-control crumbling steadily.

During my confusion, Izzy got up from the sofa. "He wants us to, you know," she whispered.

"P-Pardon?"

Her eyes bore into mine. "Danny…he wants us…to make love."

"Izzy, I don't think—"

You know you want her…

The cursed voice was right. I did want her. In fact, I'd never wanted a woman more in my life. But I also knew what a terrible mistake that would be. No matter how much I wanted her, I just couldn't take advantage of a grieving woman.

She wants you to, dammit…

It doesn't matter. I just can't do it, so get the hell out of my head!

"I can tell you don't want to." She'd lowered her head.

"What?"

"Danny just told me…you don't want to."

My God... The voice was communicating with *both* of us. But was it really Danny Glen? Or was it my own inner self warning me about doing the unforgivable?

*You've got to believe in some*thing...

A shiver inched its way up my back. I fought to stay in control.

"You don't, do you?" she asked in a whisper.

"Izzy, it's not that at all."

"What *is* it?"

"I don't know. This is so...so damned *weird...*"

She shrugged. "That doesn't mean that it's wrong, does it?"

"I think it is."

"Why is it?"

"I'd be taking advantage of you."

She took a breath. "Maybe I *want* you to take advantage of me. If Danny wants you to and if I want you to, maybe it's right that you do. Maybe you're meant to do it. Maybe you were meant to all along..."

I told you she wants you to...

You're telling her to, dammit. And she's listening to you!

It doesn't matter, does it?

Yes. It matters. It matters a great deal!

"I can tell you don't want to." She'd obviously sensed something coming from me, but I was reasonably sure she couldn't tell what was in my heart. Sighing tiredly, she went over to the front door.

You idiot.

175

I have principles, dammit!
Others would call them hang-ups.

I ignored that last remark and followed her to the door. I wanted to tell her how I truly felt but realized that wouldn't matter. She was preoccupied with having sex with me because of what she imagined Danny Glen was telling her. She obviously didn't want to hear anything else.

"I didn't mean to…to make you feel…well, to upset you," she said, looking up at me.

"I know."

"I want you to know…I don't walk up to other men and do this. I *never* do this. I've always been faithful to Danny. I could never…I'm really not that way."

"I just wish I could make you understand how I feel about this…about you…about—"

"You're a good man, Brad. That's probably why Danny chose you."

That statement alone made me feel worse than I ever thought imaginable. "I don't *feel* so good right now…"

She moved closer and brushed my cheek with the palm of her hand. Her touch was very warm. It made my skin tingle. Her face was less than a foot away, and I realized right then that I'd never wanted to kiss a woman so much before in my entire life.

"I'm sorry," she said softly. "I…didn't mean to touch you. It's just that—"

"No one has *ever* touched me like that before…" The inside of my mouth had gone dry.

The silence grew hot and unbearable. I felt like a kid on Prom Night taking my date, the homecoming queen, to her front door while wondering if I should even attempt to kiss her.

"Brad?"

"Yes?"

"Are you all right? You've got a funny look on your face."

"I do feel kind of funny right now."

"Do you need to sit down?"

"It's not *that* kind of funny…" I couldn't take my eyes off her mouth.

"What is it? The rum?"

A shiver rippled through me. "It's not the rum."

"What is it, then?"

I took in a deep breath and felt my heart sputter.

"Brad? What is—"

"It's you."

She didn't reply. Her eyes lowered and she began staring at my mouth. I knew right then that I couldn't take much more of this. I could tell that in just a few minutes, no matter how hard I resisted, I was going to be in bed with this woman.

She continued staring at me. Tears had gathered in her eyes, glittering under the foyer lighting. She began trembling.

"Izzy?" I moved closer to her. "Is there something…something I can do?"

Her eyes grew as she watched me. A tear trickled down her cheek.

"Izzy?"

"I really think Danny wants us to…"

"I know."

"But you don't want to because…because you don't think it's right?"

I glanced at her neck and visualized attacking it with my lips and tongue. "That's not exactly what's going through my mind right now."

She blinked, and more tears drifted down her cheeks. "Then…are you saying you want to?"

I closed my eyes and tried once more to hold everything in but found that I could no longer do it. I felt both weak and ready to lose control.

"Brad? *Please* tell me what you're—"

"Izzy…" My pulse raced.

"Talk to me, Brad. Please?"

"Izzy, I never wanted a woman so much before in my—"

Without warning, she stepped closer, pressing her body against me and wrapping her arms around my neck. I could feel the intense heat emanating from her, and I shivered as my body heated up as well. "Izzy…"

"*Sshhh*…"

"I really don't think—"

"You want me, don't you?" Her mouth was less than an inch from mine. I could smell the vanilla in her hair.

"We really shouldn't—"

Her warm lips mashed against mine. As we kissed, I closed my eyes and welcomed the warm, intense darkness caressing us both. I could also hear that strange voice somewhere inside me, calling to

178

me from some distant place: *We belong to each other, baby, and nothing can keep us apart...*

The heat and the intense darkness increased. As our bodies pressed harder against one another, my thoughts began looping. I could have sworn I felt myself pulling away. For one brief instant, I sensed someone else with us...someone who'd emerged from the darkness within me and moved closer to Izzy. The darkness intensified, and Izzy disappeared. A jolt of cold climbed up my back. My lips still clung to hers, but I no longer saw her face. A moment later, her image returned, but I no longer felt her lips on mine.

Just then, she pulled away and gasped. Her face remained only an inch from mine as she whispered, "You'll always be mine, Danny..."

Before I could respond, her lips pressed hotly to mine again, but I still could no longer feel her kiss. A heavy wave of dizziness had swept up from the floor. Another thick cloak of darkness swept over me. Then we were clinging to one another and devouring each other.

However, something was very wrong. I seemed to be *watching* the festivities rather than *participating* in them. I had no feeling whatsoever of Izzy's body...or even my own.

The room began spinning. Everything turned hot and hazy. Images swam before my eyes—faces and things I'd never seen before. As I gazed at Izzy gasping and squirming beneath me, I had a nagging feeling that some strange force had been unleashed inside me and taken over.

"Make love to me, Danny…take me…consume me!"

"I'm…not Danny…" I could barely hear my own voice.

"Love me, Danny!"

"I'm not…" And then my voice disappeared.

The voice inside me began speaking again. It seemed much closer, and as it spoke, I felt my composure—as well as my self-control—crumbling quickly.

"I'm back," the voice said. "I've come back for you, baby…"

"I knew you would, Danny…I just knew it!"

"We're together again, baby…"

"Come to me, Danny…*come to me!*"

I opened my mouth to tell her once again that I wasn't Danny—that she was hallucinating—but my mind immediately went blank, and my thoughts began spinning around frantically again. Music filled my ears, and I watched in confusion as I pulled away from Izzy. I didn't *want* to pull away but sensed that the same strange force that had taken over was the one behind all this.

Izzy began fading. Her image was soon smothered by the darkness. The music continued. As the darkness grew thicker, I discovered that I was no longer making love to Izzy. I was trudging through the grass in the darkness.

Moments later, the music grew softer—as if it had faded into the darkness as well. Then, when the music finally ebbed and turned into a heavy silence, the darkness erupted into a cascade of bright colors

180

rushing at me. With the colors came an explosion of brightness that gradually faded away.

When the brightness cleared, I discovered that I was standing in the middle of a hilly orchard. Trees stood everywhere, extending into the darkness. The grass, thick and soft, had a dark tint to it, possibly due to the darkness smothering this place. The lush hill behind me was covered with a thin veil of darkness. The hill rose to a height of about a hundred feet at roughly a thirty-five-degree angle. A slim, dark figure stood at the very top, looking down at me. The figure was so far away that I couldn't make out its features. I couldn't even tell if it was male or female. The moment our eyes met, it raised its right arm and waved.

I scurried up the hill. To my amazement, I found that ascending it was ridiculously easy. I wasn't even slightly winded by the time I reached the top. But my elation was short-lived as I drew closer to the figure and saw its face. The moment I realized who I was looking at, an explosion of fear slammed into me.

The figure was Danny Glen.

Chapter 23

"Recognize me?" Danny Glen asked, grinning.

There was no doubt. This was definitely the man I'd accidentally killed on Colonial Drive.

Yet he was alive… I'd killed him, but now he was *alive*…

I had to clear my throat to find my voice. Even so, the words came out weakly. "You're…Danny Glen…"

"That's right, my man. Good guess."

"But you're…you *can't* be…how can you possibly be—"

"Be what, dude? Alive? Not dead anymore? Standing upright? Talking to you?"

"Well…yes!"

"Weird, wouldn't you say?"

"I just can't believe you're actually…I can't believe—"

"Believe it, man. I'm the dude you turned into roadkill." His glazed grin made me wonder if he was drunk. Then I remembered: he *was* drunk when I'd killed him. He was drunk and high on coke.

What was going on? Where the hell were we? And why was he standing here, alive again and in the same drunken state he'd been in when I ran into him?

"Sorry about the attitude, but it isn't every day you meet up with the jerk that killed you."

I couldn't believe it. I was facing Danny Glen, the man I'd killed just a couple of days earlier.

There he was, standing right in front of me, grinning like a crazy man.

This made absolutely no sense. I'd *killed* this man. If he was dead, how in heaven's name could he be able to talk to me?

What *was* this place? Had I died as well? The last thing I recalled was lying in my bed, making love to Izzy...

"Make love to me, Danny...take me...consume me..."

"I've come back for you, baby..."

Then I remembered. As Izzy and I made love, everything turned dark, and dizziness swept over me... Numbness took over, and I no longer felt Izzy's body. Then I heard Danny's voice in my head, telling her he was coming back—

Coming back? How the hell could he come back?

The man was dead. How could he—

"Confused?" The man's glazed grin made me nervous.

"Where...*are* we?" I gazed stupidly at the solid wall of darkness behind him.

"Where do you think?"

"I have no idea. I only know you're dead. I killed you."

"Sure did, dude. I vividly remember flyin' in the air when your fancy ride slammed into me. You splattered me all over the highway."

It was getting increasingly difficult to ignore his glib attitude.

"Then...if you're dead...what am *I*?"

"You're with me—couldn't you figure that one out by yourself?"

I refused to believe I was dead. The important question was why I was no longer in my bedroom with Izzy.

"Where the hell *are* we?"

He shrugged. "Guess."

"I wish I could."

"As I just said, man, you're with me." He chuckled. "And if *I'm* dead, then do the math..."

That made no sense at all. I was in bed with Izzy. The only explanation for my death would be that she'd killed me. Or maybe I'd suffered a massive coronary. But I couldn't remember anything like that happening. All I remembered was the dizziness that took over while we were making love, the coldness creeping down my back and the darkness enveloping me, and no longer feeling her lips on my own... And, of course, suddenly pulling away from her even though I didn't want to.

Had I actually died without knowing it?

"How can I be dead?"

"Maybe you're not..."

"Then where *is* this place? And why am I here?"

"I guess you could say I kinda switched things around. I did it while you were otherwise occupied and distracted, of course. Otherwise, you might've noticed and messed it all up. But thanks to Izzy—"

"Switched things *around*?" I still didn't understand what happened and found it impossible

184

to grasp what he was telling me. However, his tone suggested that I might not want to hear the rest of it.

"You killed me, but here I am—and so are you. We're kind of in the same boat, one could say. Get it now?"

"No. I *don't* get it…"

"Let me put it this way: we needed to have a long chat, and I was the only one who was able to make the arrangements."

"A *chat*?"

He shrugged. "Like we're havin' right now. You know, you talk, and I listen, then I talk, and you listen… Then *voila*! A chat is born."

I still didn't understand.

He shook his head. "You still don't get it, do ya, boss?"

I gazed at the darkness of the hills and the trees until everything meshed together. Then it dawned on me—none of this was real. It was all in my mind—my imagination.

"This feels almost like a dream… You're not really here, are you? And if you aren't, neither am I."

"No dream, dude. This is the real thing. And believe me—both of us are really here."

"But how'd this happen?"

"You made it happen yourself, man."

"Me?"

He chuckled. "You and your guilt."

"My *what*?"

"You felt so guilty about mowin' me down, you turned into a basket case—and also a seriously soft touch."

"My *guilt* brought me here?"

"What else could it have been? I'm not some flashy supernatural dude, ya know. I'm just a guy who knows how to play a damn good trumpet."

"But where *are* we? What *is* this place? Is it really death?"

"It would've been—for me, anyway—but you were so torn up about everything, you changed the game plan. And when I finally figured out what was goin' on, I did my own planning and decided to use you to get back."

What in heaven's name did he mean by that?

"I...don't understand."

"You kept summonin' me, dude. Callin' me. Talkin' to me. Thinkin' about me. Then you got Izzy involved." He shook his head. "That was a *really* bad move, my good man. That babe's been studyin' the supernatural, seein' ghosts and sniffin' out dead people since she was a little brat. I love her half to death, but she's got this intuition thing that can really bum the crap out of a guy. Anyway, you got her all wired up, and when she gets radical about somethin', all hell breaks loose."

"This is *my* fault?"

"That's the rumor."

"It sounds so...so—"

"Freaky? Yeah, it does. But since you started the ball rollin', dude, I figured I'd experiment a little and see how far I could take it. I started havin' some fun with you—not much, but just enough to let me see how things would go. First thing I did, I decided to see if I could get you to take us to Raymond's. That's where you met the guys—and, of course, Izzy."

This was beginning to make sense. "*You* were the one who actually lured me there?"

He nodded. "Granted, I can't drive or steer..." He held up his hands. "You kinda took that power away from me. But it didn't take that much for me to guide you on the right path. Since I had your total attention, I found it really easy—and great fun—to get you to make the right turns."

"But why?"

A shrug. "I needed you and Izzy to hook up. I figured she'd be my trump card. And, of course, the guys had Bessie."

"Bessie?"

"My horn. I had to see how fucked up she was. I was real pleased there wasn't a mark on her. That extra foam padding I'd stitched into my gig bag a few years back made a difference."

The realization made me want to grind my teeth. "If I hadn't gone there..."

"You wouldn't have met Izzy. Guess I did us both a favor, eh, dude?"

I couldn't believe this was happening.

"I also got you to take your coffee black. That worked like a charm, too. So since I was on a serious roll, I decided to keep on goin'. That's why you went to the Mall and bought some of my favorite CDs. Then, of course, the rum and Coke thingy. By the way, in case you haven't figured it out by now, I hate Scotch." He grimaced.

"I thought I was going crazy."

He grinned. "And whaddya think now?"

"I'm either crazy...or dead."

"See there? You're not as stupid as you think."

I ignored the remark. There were more crucial things at stake. I was even more determined than ever to find out what was going on so I could try and make things right again. "But how were you able to do all *this*? Getting me here?"

"No idea, dude, but as the old sayin' goes, if it works, don't fix it."

"*You* brought Izzy to my condo, didn't you?"

Danny Glen chuckled. "Ya think she would've found you so quickly on her own?"

I was growing more and more enraged. This was all so cruel. And his attitude only made things worse. "But why? Why'd you do it? Why'd you send her to my place?"

"I knew she'd be able to put this all together with her sensitivity shtick, so I had you seduce her. I figured that by usin' her as a kind of medium, I just might be able to squeeze through."

"Squeeze through?"

"As I've been tryin' to say, dude, you haven't left me alone at all. You kept me right there."

"Right where?"

He jabbed a finger at my chest. "Right there. With you."

"But you're *here*—wherever *here* is..." The darkness surrounding us prevented me from seeing anything but the spot of dark ground beneath our feet and the blurred mass of trees at the bottom of the hill.

"I know, but even though I was here, I was also really close to you. I can't figure out exactly where that was, but you somehow made it even closer with that guilt thingy you've been cartin' around on your shoulders. I don't know if this is some alternate universe or what. I couldn't do any worthwhile explorin' of the place. I tried goin' into the woods a few times, but you kept callin' me. And each time you called, it felt as if you were actually pullin' me back in this direction."

"I don't remember doing that."

"You might not have done it consciously, but each time I tried walkin' down this hill or gettin' closer to those woods, I felt a strong tug, so I couldn't go anywhere but come back here. I figured it was you pullin' me back. It seemed that everywhere I turned, there you were—or your aura, or whatever the hell you wanna call it—and the more you agonized over me, the closer you got, and the clearer I could see you. See, I never really believed in any of that spiritual mumbo-jumbo Izzy loves so much. I never believed in it until you ran me over and sent me here." He laughed. "Guess what? I believe in it now. And I guess I was right about your guilt thingy. You're here with me, aren't ya?"

"But—"

"And guess what else? While we're both here at the same time, I think we're gonna pull a slight switcheroo for a little while."

"P-Pardon me?"

He held out his hands and chuckled. "I'm pullin' a fancy presto-chango!"

"A what?"

"From now on, I'm Brad Ellis!"

"What are you talking about?"

"Listen, dude…while you're takin' the time to figure this all out, I could be back there, havin' a ball with Izzy and the guys. I really miss playin' to a live audience. I've been playin' here, on top of this hill, but I'm kind of isolated—know what I mean? I can make Bessie appear when I want, so that's really no problem. This place seems to be all mental—you know, sort of dream-like—but I can still make some damn good tones. Even so, playin' out here in the middle of nowhere gets a tad boring after a while. So, if ya don't mind, I'll just squeeze on through and let you do your thing here for a while—get what I'm sayin'?"

"No! I *don't* get what you're saying!" The panic in me flared up, telling me he was about to do something unconscionable. I had to get him to reconsider whatever he had on his mind. "If you'll just take it easy so we can talk about this—"

"Later, dude. I've got things to do. Besides, I've gotta get back before Izzy realizes I'm gone. Right now, she's probably gettin' her beauty sleep after that last romp." He chuckled. "We both gave her quite a time, didn't we? Anyway, gotta go. Don't forget to write!"

Then, before I realized what he'd just said, he disappeared.

It didn't register at first, but moments later, the horrible reality of the situation finally came to me. I told myself that I was imagining all this. He couldn't actually do what he'd just done. He couldn't switch spirits and take over my mortal form as if he'd merely changed clothes.

No one could do that, could they?

"Danny?" I stared at the empty space in the grass where he'd been standing moments ago. Then I turned around and gazed numbly at the slope of the long hill just a few yards in front of me.

Only the heavy silence told me what I feared.

I was standing all alone at the top of a hill in a strange world filled with darkness. And I had no idea how I could possibly escape.

Chapter 24

Just as I was about to venture down the hill, I heard Izzy's voice.

It sounded very close and seemed to be coming from an area just a foot or so directly above me. I looked up but all I saw was darkness.

"Danny, is it you? Is it really you?"

"Who else would it be, baby?" His voice came from the same place. It sounded like my voice, and it sliced into me like a machete. "Who else could rock your world like that?"

"No one, Danny, no one. It was *so* wonderful..."

"Yeah, it was pretty damn far out."

"Danny, what's going on?"

"Going on?"

"You were dead, but now...you've come back..."

"I'm not dead, baby. I just proved it, didn't I?" A chuckle.

"But you were, weren't you?"

"If I was, how'd I come back? You don't come back from the dead, ya know. Not unless you're a zombie, and we both know zombies aren't real, right?"

Silence.

"Baby? You know I'm right, don'tcha?"

More silence.

"Baby?"

"Danny, where *were* you?"

"Whaddya mean?"

"You were gone. Now you're here. Something just isn't right…"

"Can't you tell this is me, baby?"

"I *wish* I could…"

"What's wrong?"

"Danny, your voice…"

"What about it?"

"It's…different…"

Silence.

"Danny? Did you hear me?"

"I heard ya, baby."

"Sometimes you sound like Brad…and other times—"

"Other times I sound like me, right?"

Silence.

"Right, baby?"

"It's really strange, Danny. When I look at you, you sound like Brad…but when I close my eyes, you sound just like your old self."

"Sorry, baby, but as I told ya a hundred times before, I can't tell what's goin' on in that pretty little head."

Silence.

"Baby?"

"Danny, you look totally different. How can that be?"

"Does it make any difference? I'm back. That's all that should really matter."

"I don't know, Danny. I'm so confused. You're here and Brad's gone. Just a few minutes ago, Brad was right here. Now he's gone and you're here. I like Brad. He's a really nice guy who came to the club the other night. He came to offer his—oh my God…"

"What's wrong, baby?"

Silence.

"Baby?"

"Danny…where have you *been*? When you left Vizzutti's the other night… What happened?"

"I was gonna go back to the pad, just like I always do after a gig. You know that."

"I only know you were in no shape to drive."

"I didn't drive. I walked. Don't you remember? You took my keys and hid 'em. You didn't want me to drive. And since you wouldn't give me back my damn keys, I had to get home a different way. I stayed in the dressing room a little too long. Bill wanted me to ride home with him, but I was doin' a line of quality stuff and wanted to stay a while longer. When I finally left, no one else was around to give me a ride, so I started walkin'. There was this cab parked off Colonial, so I—"

"You had all that rum, Danny. You shouldn't have even tried to—"

"Baby, I don't wanna go through this shit anymore. Sure, I had a lot to drink, but that really doesn't matter, does it? Not anymore."

"You also had too much snort."

"Dammit, it helps me unwind. I'm all geared up after a couple of sets and have to wind down. I get the shakes and can't settle down. Blow's great for that. You know that."

194

"I know you weren't in any condition to leave the club that night, period."

"But I did. I managed even though you took my damn keys away. You know how I feel about that infernal nagging."

"I wasn't nagging, Danny. I was concerned. You know how I get, how I worry about you—"

"Yeah, yeah. I know all about your problems, baby."

"They're not *problems*, Danny. They're concerns. I really and truly love you. When two people love one another—"

"I know, baby. I know."

"So what happened that night?"

"As I just said, I headed straight for the cab across the street. Where else would I have—"

"You didn't get that far, did you?"

"Are ya tryin' to say you think I'm cheatin' on ya, baby?"

"That's not what I'm saying *at all*!"

"What *are* you sayin'?"

"Danny…what's the last thing you remember?"

"I grabbed Bessie, left Vizzutti's and started walkin' down the street. Then…"

"Then what?"

"I can't remember, baby. I…I was ready to cross Colonial. I saw the cab sittin' in the parkin' lot across the street in front of that coffee shop. The cabby was inside on a stool, having coffee. I figured I could get a ride home, but…"

"But what, Danny?"

195

"I saw all these really far-out bright lights…and then…"

"Go on, Danny. I need to know."

"There were all these bright lights comin' at me, and I couldn't move. The lights…they were so cool, so beautiful, I just wanted to stand there and watch 'em. I actually heard music when I saw 'em. *That's* what happened, baby. I heard music, and this strange ballad-like melody, and I was tryin' to piece it all together into a new song when the lights went all kinds of funny. Then everything went dark, and I felt this terrific pain in my knees. Then I looked up and saw that Bessie and I were flyin' in the air. I heard more music, and then I felt myself fallin'. The whole thing was really far out—"

"Danny…"

"What, baby?"

"You died that night."

Silence.

"Did you hear me, Danny?"

More silence.

"Danny? Did you—"

"I heard ya, baby."

"You understand what I'm saying, don't you?"

Silence.

"Danny?"

"Baby, all ya need to be concerned about is—"

"You died. I know you did."

"Baby, I was in some weird place you go before you die. I was obviously in some sort of a coma. A blow to my head put me in a coma. It

196

prob'ly happened when I landed on the road. But I snapped out of it, and now we're together again—"

"Danny—"

"I don't think I actually *died*, baby—not the way ya think, anyway. The dude that hit me put me into a coma, and I went to this weird place and stayed there for a little while."

"What sort of weird place?"

"It was, well...ya know, I really can't remember it right now. I do remember that it was dark, but I guess I was too zoned out to remember the details. I remember wanderin' around, lookin' for a way back, and that's when I kept hearin' this dude talkin' to me, tellin' me how sorry he was that he'd run me over. He wouldn't leave me alone, so I couldn't find my way back. Every damn time I tried looking for a way back, there he was, apologizin', distractin' me."

"Who hit you, Danny?"

"That Ellis guy. I thought ya already knew."

"*Brad* hit you?"

"It wasn't his fault, baby. I was kinda askin' for it, the way I just stood there like a shithead. Couldn't help it, though... Like I said, those lights were really far out. They were friggin' beautiful. Anyhow, it no longer matters, does it? I'm back."

"It wasn't just some weird place, Danny. You died. The police called and had me come in. They even gave me your gig bag."

Silence.

"Danny, did you hear what I just said?"

"It couldn't have happened like that, baby. You just can't come back once you actually die. True, I'd been trippin'. I had a lot to drink, and then the coke later on. Everything went all screwy on me. But as I keep tellin' ya, I saw all those bright lights and heard this song, and then the lights were awfully close, and everything exploded. I must've tripped out, because right after, I was wanderin' around in this weird dark place. I must've been in a coma. Nothin' else makes any—"

"You're dead, Danny."

A chuckle. "How can that be, baby? We just messed up the sheets like mad. You were right there with me. Look at you. You're still right here with me."

"I know what we just did, but something's not right."

"What's wrong, baby? I thought I just rocked your world."

"Oh, Danny…"

"Baby, ya know you're actin' weird, don'tcha?"

"I don't think you really know what's happened."

"Sure I do. I just told ya. I had too damn much to drink, and I went a little heavy on the snort…but ya know how I hate anyone naggin' me. I'm thirty years old, dammit, and I don't need anyone—especially my lady—tellin' me what I can and can't—"

"You're dead, Danny!"

198

"Why do ya keep sayin' that? I'm here. We just made it. What other proof do ya need?"

"Those lights you saw. They were the headlights of the car that ran you down!"

"Baby, I know what happened, believe me. I had a nasty hit on the head and was out of it for a day or so. But I'm back, and that's all that matters, isn't it? You brought me back—you and that weird stuff you've been studyin' all these years. I don't know how ya did it, but you did, and now that I'm back, we're gonna have some fun—"

"Danny, *please*…"

"Baby, what's wrong? Why aren't you happy about all this? This is me. I'm Danny—the dude who's been rockin' your world for nearly half your life."

"Get up, Danny."

"Huh?"

"Get up. Go over to the bureau and look at yourself in the mirror."

"Baby? What the hell—"

"Just do it!"

Silence.

Moments later: "Wow…I actually *do* look just like that Ellis dude…"

"Why is that, Danny?"

A brief silence.

"Danny?"

"Baby, it doesn't matter how I look. This is me. This is Danny. I may look like Ellis, but I'm the real article. In fact—"

"I know it's you, Danny. I can tell."

"Then why all this bullshit? Why can't you just accept the fact that I've come back?"

"Because it just doesn't make any sense!"

"What doesn't?"

"Any of it!"

"Listen, baby…why should you even care what happened? I'm back—isn't that enough?"

"Danny, *please* tell me what's going on. What really happened? Where were you? Where's Brad? What did you do with him?"

"I'll tell ya all about it one of these days."

"I'd like to know right now, Danny!"

"Baby, I don't know…why you keep…" His voice began fading.

"Danny…I don't think…happening…" Izzy's voice also began to fade.

"Baby…weird…seriously…far out…"

"This is…"

I could no longer hear either of them.

The dead silence slammed into me.

Chapter 25

As my mind swam with crazy images, I found that I was much too numb to move.

In spite of my urge to descend the hill to begin exploring my new surroundings, I remained at the crest, gazing fearfully at the pine forest awaiting me in a huge, blurred mass of darkness just beyond the foot of the hill.

I struggled to maintain my composure, but I was just so overwhelmed by the insanity of events that I couldn't concentrate. I took several deep breaths, closed my eyes, and struggled to think clearly.

When I thought I was finally making progress, I forced the panic away and fought to start thinking rationally. However, my hopelessness quickly intervened, and I had to face the fact that my existence had evaporated before my very eyes. Although I hadn't actually died, I was no longer among the living. Instead, I was stuck in a strange world I never even knew existed. The man I'd accidentally killed had somehow tricked me, sabotaging my spirit and using my physical body to return to the land of the living.

How on earth had this happened?

Had Danny Glen been right about all this? Had he been right about *any* of it? Had my guilt betrayed me? Was the sympathy and grief I'd felt for killing him the prime factor that had enabled him to steal my existence from me?

I couldn't believe this had happened. I just couldn't believe that I'd let the spirit of a dead man take over my mortal body.

Izzy knew what had happened. She might not have known what was going on, but when Danny Glen had seemingly returned from the dead, she must have figured out at least *some* of it. She was bright and perceptive and, hopefully, quite rational. She'd understand what happened. And she wouldn't accept it because it was against everything she believed and loved.

But would she *do* something about it?

More importantly, what *could* she do?

***

Once I had the panic somewhat under control, I knew what had to be done. I had to do whatever I could to appeal to Danny Glen's sense of decency. For this, it would be necessary for me to communicate with him again. It seemed logical to me that, if he'd been able to communicate with me from this place, I should be able to do the same thing with him. It didn't matter that the circumstances were now reversed. I refused to believe that he felt no guilt for what he'd just done. I was prepared to use that as a bargaining chip to coax him to do the right thing.

Taking a few deep breaths, I closed my eyes, focused, and summoned every bit of concentration I had within me to send a message to him. "Danny, you need to talk to me…"

I waited. I heard nothing.

I focused even harder on his image. "Danny, this is not right."

Still nothing.

"Danny, I demand that you speak to me this instant!"

More silence.

As I struggled to stay in control, I distracted myself from letting the anger take over by thinking about my next message. Since he might very well be ignoring me, I couldn't try bullying him, and I certainly couldn't prompt a conversation by making him feel guilty. Gentleness might work better. I had to be gentle. And I had to make him think I didn't hate him for what he did or would want revenge. It would be difficult, but I had to work it this way.

Just as I was about to send my message, I heard his voice: "Whaddya want, dude?"

My heart raced. I took another deep breath and told myself to do whatever was necessary to keep the anger and the self-pity as far away as possible, at least for now. I had to proceed calmly and rationally. For now, he held all the aces. If I upset or aggravated him, he'd simply switch me off. "I believe you know what I want."

After a long silence, he chuckled—which raked on my nerves. "I'll bet you think I'm pretty much of an asshole right now."

It took every bit of self-control I had in me to keep from telling him he was absolutely right. *Stay focused. Proceed calmly and rationally.* "I'll gladly change my opinion if you decide to do the right thing."

"And that would be…?"

"You know what I'm talking about."

"Hmmm… I'm guessin' you're prob'ly keen on the two of us switchin' things back, right?"

"That would be the most humane thing to do, wouldn't it?"

"Listen, dude... You killed me, remember? You took away all that I was and all I'd ever be. You can prob'ly already tell that I'm not exactly seein' things your way right now, can ya?"

"Listen, Danny…I know I killed you, but you also know it was an accident."

"Sure. I know ya didn't mean it. But that doesn't really change anything now, does it?"

"Danny, you were drunk…and you'd done cocaine…"

"Dude, everyone needs to relax—know what I mean? I'd just done four long sets at Vizzutti's. Ever been there?"

"I really don't know what this has to do with—"

"It's a tough room, man—especially the after-dinner crowd. Half those idiots go there to get drunk while the other half listens to the band, dances a little and *then* gets drunk. The ones who go there alone hope to get laid, but that's a whole different ball game. Anyway, you've got more than a hundred drunks staggerin' around, doin' stupid things on the dance floor. Meanwhile, the really smashed assholes are tryin' to climb the stage. The ones who don't make it up the steps usually fall and knock over a bunch of other assholes. That almost always starts a fight, and then it takes quite a while to get the room back under control. Now…the ones who *do* reach the stage? That's an even scarier scenario. Some of those assholes are so drunk that they think it's Karaoke Night, and they try and snatch the mike so they can sing for their drunken friends. The others—the ones too drunk to sing?—they go for the instruments, because everyone knows that when you're drunk, it means you need to grab an instrument and try and play music, right? Anyway, even if they don't make it to the instruments, they'd knock over the mikes, the sound equipment and the speakers if we didn't stop 'em."

"Danny—"

"Listen, man… Bits of Jazz is a damn good group, but sometimes the crowds get to ya, and pullin' in a line or two after a gig is the only way a player's got to deal with the bullshit without freakin' out—get me?"

"I understand. I really do, but—"

"If you're cool with it, then ya know why I was so stoned that night."

"Yes. I do. But that doesn't mean—"

"Good, my man. I'm glad ya feel me."

"I do feel you. I really do. But that doesn't give you the right to—"

"Dude, I made it back, okay? Life's cool again. Izzy and I are back together, and tomorrow I'm goin' over to her pad and pick up Bessie. I really miss her. The band's got a gig booked for tomorrow night, and I've got to get back with 'em and let 'em know I'm still alive—know what I mean?"

"You just can't *do* this!" I felt as if I was about to explode inside.

"I can, dude. I have to, because that's who I am. And when the guys see that I'm back, things'll be cool again. It'll take 'em a little time gettin' used to your looks and all, but once they're cool with who I really am inside—"

"You have to give me back my life!" The heat growing inside me had become unbearable.

"Sorry, dude. You took mine away, so why shouldn't ya give it back if the opportunity presents itself?"

"This isn't fair!"

"Neither was what ya did to me, but things are pretty well square now, so why quibble?"

"They're *not* square! They'll never *be* square— not as long as things stay the way they are!"

"Depends on how ya look at it, dude. Before, they weren't square with *me*, but now, they're not square with *you*. *Quid pro quo*, as ol' Hannibal Lecter would say—right, Clarisse?" A chuckle.

The sound of his laughter ripped through me. "This isn't right!"

"Chill, dude. That place ain't that bad, ya know. Didn't ya hear me playin' while you were down here, feelin' all guilty and messed up about runnin' me over?"

"What does that have to do with—"

"It has a lot to do with it. It's really cool there, actually. You imagine somethin' and suddenly it's right there. I just imagined Bessie in my hands again, and *voila*! There I was, playin' just as if I was down here all along! Far out, man!"

"But—"

"I take it you don't play?"

"Of *course* I don't play! What would make you think—"

"You can prob'ly learn a bunch of things while you're there, dude. I don't remember much about that place, but that's only because you wouldn't leave me alone long enough to figure out what it actually was. But I was able to play even though I didn't bring Bessie with me. Doesn't that tell ya it's a really great place?"

"I don't *belong* here!"

"You'll get used to it."

"I'm not dead! I don't *have* to get used to it! *You're* the one who's dead! *You're* the one has to—"

"Don't forget to write."

"Danny, you can't just *leave* me here!"

Silence.

"Dammit, Danny! *Talk* to me!"

Nothing.

He'd stopped listening and switched off. And I was totally alone once again.

Chapter 26

I lingered at the crest of the grassy hill, trembling and cursing myself for letting this nightmare happen. I was angry, hurt and depressed, and wanted to scream my lungs out as the cold terror clung to me like some ghastly disease.

I wanted to go back in time—just as I'd felt after the highway accident. This time, however, things would be different. I wanted to go back not *just before* I'd slammed into Danny Glen, but *right after*, when my guilt first started taking over.

If only I *could* go back...

I knew I'd still feel badly about the accident, but I certainly wouldn't let the guilt consume me. I'd fight it this time. And I certainly wouldn't listen to strange voices in my head.

You have no control over your feelings...

Yes. I knew that. But if I knew then what was going to happen, I would have tried much harder to keep all my unwanted baggage under wraps.

You honestly think you would have done that?

Yes. I honestly do.

It's a real shame that you can't go back, isn't it?

Once that frightening realization slammed into me, I decided that since I couldn't go back, I might as well try to move forward. If Danny had been right about this strange world being "really cool," I decided that while I was stranded here, I should at least do a little exploring to see what I could find.

I started walking back down the hill. I had no idea in which direction I should go once I reached the bottom; I just knew that I couldn't stand at the crest much longer and continue feeling sorry for myself. It wouldn't accomplish anything.

But what *could* I accomplish in this strange world?

I had no clue. Other than Danny telling me that everything was "mental" here, and that he'd produced his trumpet just by thinking about it, I didn't know how that would help me return to the world of the living. Could I produce a cell phone? Even if I was able to, who could I call? Gloria? Izzy? And if I did, what could they do? How could they help me?

More importantly, would I be able to get a signal?

Suddenly curious, I stopped descending the hill. Although I felt like an idiot for doing so, I held out my hand, closed my eyes and visualized the image of a cell phone lying flat in my palm.

About half a minute later, I opened my eyes. My palm was empty.

My depression came roaring back.

I shoved the darkness aside. Depression had no place in my thoughts right now. The fact that someone had done this to me in the first place kept the anger uncomfortably close. Even so, I was determined not to let it consume me. I had to figure a way out of this. Otherwise, I was stuck here.

But where was *here*? What *was* this place?

It didn't matter, did it? It didn't matter what Danny said about it or what it really was. The only thing that did matter was that it wasn't *my* place. I didn't belong here.

I fully realized this was a hopelessly desperate predicament, but I couldn't let it destroy me. I couldn't give up. If I did, I had to face the fact that I'd have to spend eternity wandering around helplessly in this strange place.

But what could I do? How could I get back when the man responsible for bringing me here refused to talk to me?

Once I reached the bottom of the hill, I headed for the pine forest straight ahead. I had no idea what lay beyond the darkness among the trees but knew I had to keep moving. As long as I remained active, my mind continued to function, and as long as my mental processes kept working, I might eventually come up with a plan.

I finally reached the tree line. Although the darkness hovering just beyond them was impenetrable, I sensed that I was following some sort of trail. A trail meant someone else had been here. It also meant that if I kept walking, I might stumble upon them.

Then what?

I had no idea.

I suddenly stopped moving and for nearly a minute thought about turning around. Then I thought of the hill. I really had no choice but continue walking away from it. Despite who—or what—had used this trail before me, I had to keep moving.

Alert for deadfalls, I kept my eyes focused on the darkness directly in front of me and held my arms out in front of me to protect my face from hanging moss and dangling branches. I maintained a slow, steady pace, my ears pricked for sounds other than those my feet were making.

As I continued my journey, I calculated that I'd probably covered close to half of a mile. Suddenly tired and even more discouraged than ever, I stopped walking and turned around. When I saw nothing but total darkness enveloping me, the terror came back. The realization was quite clear. I had to forget about what I'd left behind me and resume my journey.

Taking a deep breath and forcing the terror away once again, I resumed walking. After another ten minutes or so, I felt a little hope nudging me as I approached the tree line at the opposite end of the woods. The darkness ended just beyond it, and a hazy gray fog distinguished the shadows among the trees. As I approached, one of the shadows nipped at my senses.

I stopped cold.

A tall, slender figure was standing between two giant pines, watching me.

***

Frightened and confused, I stopped walking and stood stock-still.

The sight of someone else in this mysterious place had not made me feel any better. After what

211

I'd been through in the last couple of days, I feared nothing good would ever happen to me again.

Though the figure was probably fifty yards away, I could tell I was looking at a man. Even in the hazy gray fog surrounding him, I saw that he was tall and broad-shouldered, with long, flowing white hair.

Was I looking at God?

The absurd notion made me feel like an idiot. Why would God be standing in a pine forest, watching me? This dark, frightening place couldn't possibly be Heaven. Even if it was, and this figure was indeed God, I guessed there would be angels close by, hovering in the darkness, their wings giving off a golden or silvery glow.

You're being silly.

I know, but at least I have a good reason.

Reason or not, go see the man.

It sounded logical, but I couldn't shake the suspicion that had consumed me the moment I first saw him. Who was he and what did he want? And why was he standing between two giant pines, watching me?

What have you got to lose?

This was something I hadn't considered before now. What could go wrong now? I'd lost my physical body and was wandering around blindly, searching for an escape from a strange dark world. The worst that could happen was that this stranger was actually the devil and was welcoming newcomers. I realized how silly that sounded, too, but I was frightened and much too confused to reject any lame-brained idea that came into my head.

In any event, I had to do *some*thing.

After several tries, I got my legs moving once again. I approached him cautiously, my gaze on him all the while. He didn't move. When I was about fifteen feet away, I stopped walking. The gray fog prevented me from distinguishing his features, but I could somehow make out clear blue eyes. Then he smiled and spoke. His voice was soft and soothing, like a gentle wind after a storm. "You seem hesitant and nervous," he said. "Perhaps I might be of some help…"

I didn't know if it was the tenderness in his voice, the way his eyes lit up when he spoke or his soft manner. It might have been a combination of all three. The moment I heard him speak, my suspicions vanished. So did my sense of dread.

"I really don't think I'm supposed to be here," I said, finding my voice.

"Then I take it that you have no idea where you are, do you?"

"Absolutely none."

He smiled again.

I felt myself relaxing, feeling the tension and the suspicion vanishing quickly. "You're not God, are you?" I don't know why I asked. It seemed to be the most important question in my mind right now.

He shook his head. "No, my boy. I am not. My name is Arthur."

"Then…are you dead?"

"Yes."

"How long?"

"I left my mortal body nearly eight centuries ago."

"And you've been here ever since?"

He stepped closer, and I could finally see his face. It was a handsome, fine-featured face of a man who appeared to be around fifty, with high cheekbones and a sculpted chin. He wore a long white robe which came to within an inch or two of the ground. He was probably at least three inches taller than I was, making him six-three or –four. Although his robe covered his body, I could tell by his wrists and neck that he was slender. "I go where I am needed. I was summoned here very recently. I'm summoned whenever an arriving spirit needs help. I assume you are the one needing help."

Something about all this didn't make any sense. "How would anyone know about me?"

"In this world, my boy, we are all connected, and when someone needs help, we all know immediately."

"That sounds really great. I'm gonna need all the help I can get."

"That's why I'm here."

"Well, I'm certainly glad *one* of us knows what's going on..."

"What would you like to know?"

"Let me put it this way…the only thing I *do* know is that I'm not dead."

He blinked. "Then what are you doing here?"

"You wouldn't believe me if I told you."

He went silent, contemplating me for a few moments. Then he smiled. "Son, I've seen and heard a great many things during the last eight hundred mortal years, and many of them were things a logical person just wouldn't understand or believe. But if you tell me the truth, I promise I'll believe you."

"Once you hear what I'm about to tell you, you might just consider changing your mind."

"My boy, one of my talents happens to be my ability to tell when someone is speaking the truth. And it really doesn't matter to me what the truth is or what it seems to be, just so long as it comes from the heart. Can you understand that?"

"I think so…"

He turned and gestured toward the gray fog behind him. "Let's walk, and you can tell me your story."

We slipped past the tree line.

The moment we'd stepped into the fog, everything turned bright and colorful, but appeared blurred and indistinct. Brown-shaded hills showed in the distance. Fuzzy splotches of bright colors hovered close to the ground. A hazy brook extended from the foot of the hill, with a sketchy waterfall starting at the crest, which seemed at least half a mile in the distance. The sky displayed a hazy gray. Brightness from a blurry sun cast down rays of misty gold, yellow and white. A muddled rainbow pierced another puff of white, and what might have been snow-capped mountain peaks showed like fluffy cones of dull white paint many miles from us.

I sensed that I was looking at some sort of paradise, but with a thick pane of opaque glass separating it from me.

"This is…well, beautiful." Even though I couldn't see everything clearly, I still felt overwhelmed. "But why is it so blurry?"

"You don't belong here. This alone convinces me that you've told me the truth. You can only truly see this world when you're dead."

Grainy-looking shadows were moving about in the distance. "What are those?"

"They are other spirits."

"People?"

He nodded. "We also have many horses here. They love the fresh grass. Also, dogs, cats, birds, squirrels… All sorts of happy creatures. You can't see any of them, either."

"But why I can see *you*?"

"It is because you've been displaced and need my help. You won't be able to see this place or any part of it until you've become a spirit that has left its body."

"But I *am* here. That's the problem."

"I meant, you're obviously not *scheduled* to be here. That's why you can't see this paradise. Not yet, anyway."

I suddenly found that I was tired and wanted to relax. I stopped walking. "Could we rest for a moment?"

"Certainly. You look tired, son. You've obviously had a rough time."

"I hope you won't mind if I just sit down right here for a little while…"

"Would you like a chair?"

At first I thought he was joking, but his pleasant expression didn't indicate amusement. "Are you serious?"

"Of course I'm serious."

"I'd *love* a chair right now. It seems like I've been wandering around for *hours*." I looked around. I didn't expect to see furniture out in the middle of a country setting—especially in another world. "You don't happen to have one under that robe, do you?"

Chuckling, he waved his arm. Two comfortable-looking armchairs appeared in the lush grass between us. "Will these be all right? Or would you prefer something more—"

"How did you *do* that?"

He shrugged. "I imagined them. This world is centered on the imagination and responds only to mental energy. Please. Sit."

Mental energy. This sounded like what Danny was trying to tell me.

"You imagine somethin' and suddenly it's right there…"

"You look confused, my boy."

"Can everyone here do stuff like this?"

He nodded. "In different stages, of course. It all depends on how long the spirit has been here…and, of course, how well the spirit adapts to this world."

"But I can't do anything, right?"

"Not until you truly belong here."

I nodded. "That explains why I couldn't make a cell phone."

He tilted his head. "Pardon me?"

"Don't ask."

He smiled and gestured to the chairs.

The moment my butt touched the cushion, I felt as if I really *was* in Heaven.

"Comfortable enough?"

"It's perfect." I sat back and closed my eyes. When I opened them again, I saw that he'd taken a seat in the chair facing me. He leaned forward and rested his robe-covered elbows on his thighs. "Now…I would very much like to hear your story."

Chapter 27

I told Arthur about the accident.

He didn't say a word while I spoke. Once I'd finished, he sat back and watched me in silence. I couldn't tell if he didn't believe me or thought I'd been hallucinating.

"Kind of hard to swallow, isn't it?" I finally asked.

"I've heard some strange tales in my time, but yes, it does seem like you've been dealt a particularly bad hand. What is your name, son?"

"Brad Ellis."

"And how old are you?"

That seemed a strange question, but since he was obviously here to help me, I decided not to make things worse for either or us. "I'm thirty-seven."

"And where do you live?"

Another strange question, but I assumed he knew what he was doing.

"Winter Park, Florida."

He nodded. Then he sat forward, closed his eyes, and lowered his head. After about ten seconds of silence, he began speaking to the ground at his feet. "We seem to have someone here who has paid us an unscheduled visit. His name is Brad Ellis, he's from Winter Park, Florida, and he's thirty-seven years old. Please verify."

I wanted to ask him what he was doing but didn't want to interrupt or distract him. While he was engaged in his strange communication, I scanned the area around us. At first, things remained just as I'd glimpsed them earlier. However, I noticed that some of the flowers covering the hill behind us had become slightly less opaque.

This place was beginning to reveal itself to me. It would probably become breathtakingly beautiful in no time.

About a minute later, Arthur raised his head and smiled. "It seems that you're right, Brad. You're not scheduled here for a long time to come."

I sighed in relief. "How long?"

"You're not scheduled to leave your body for another forty-two years, seven months and twenty-two days."

"That means I'll be nearly eighty when I die?"

He nodded.

It occurred to me that I shouldn't have asked such a question. Knowing the year I would die would likely jinx me for the rest of my life.

"That was stupid of me, wasn't it?"

"What was?"

"Asking when I'm supposed to die."

He smiled. "You'll soon find that it won't be much of a problem. The important thing is that you shouldn't be here in the first place."

"Well, what do I do? If I'm not dead, I shouldn't have been able to leave my body, right?"

"Right."

"But I *did*…"

He nodded.

"And because of that, I'm here, and I need to find some way of reversing what happened."

"Whatever you do, it must be done quickly. The longer you stay here, the harder it will be for you. Your spirit will relax in its new surroundings. Things will become clearer, more distinct. Right now, you can't see much—"

"I just noticed that the flowers have become clearer."

Arthur frowned. "This is bad. Your spirit is already forming an attachment to this world. It will soon become entranced, and you'll eventually lose all desire to leave. We must think of a way of getting you back so you can live out your allotted years. Otherwise, other arrangements will have to be made."

"Arrangements?"

"You could be forced to submit to the reincarnation process."

"You mean I'll have to go through this all over again?"

A nod.

"You mean, being born again? Infancy? Childhood? Adolescence? Puberty? Finding a date to the Prom again? The whole nine yards?"

"I'm afraid so…"

"Hell, no." The thoughts of going through the horrors of birth and childhood all over again made me nauseous. "Anything but that."

Arthur smiled. "You say the name of the person who tricked you is Danny Glen?"

221

"That was his professional name. His full name is Daniel Glen Morrison."

"What was his profession?"

"He was a jazz trumpeter."

He nodded. "I was informed of beautiful trumpet music coming from just beyond the pines not very long ago. That must have been this man."

"You didn't see him?"

"I wasn't here at the time. As I've said, I go where I am needed. I haven't been needed here for a great while. This Danny Glen must be an accomplished player. He'll fit in nicely with one of our bands—that is, if you can get him back here."

"I'm wondering why he didn't like it here."

"Well, since he has gone and you are here in his place, I'd say that it had something to do with you..."

"He said I distracted him."

"This, of course, directly involves the accident."

"Right after it happened, I went into serious guilt overload. I despised myself for running him down. I thought about him day and night and even dreamed about him. I began hearing voices. After talking to him, I realized that it was him communicating with me all along."

"Now I understand. You were preventing him from crossing over."

"That's basically the same thing he told me when he tricked me here to meet with him."

"This was right before he took over your mortal form, I gather?"

222

"Exactly."

"He was forced to stay out there in the darkness, beyond the boundaries of the forest. Your hold on him was much too strong to permit him to enter the woods and come out here, on the other side, where he would have crossed over to become a permanent spirit."

"So, then, if I'd let him come through the woods like he was supposed to, he'd be where we are right now and would probably love it here?"

"Yes."

"I really screwed this up, didn't I?"

Arthur smiled. "That's not what we should be focusing on right now, my boy."

"All right, so how can I get back? I *can* get back, right?"

"There are ways, yes."

A surge of warm relief washed through me. Things didn't seem so bleak or hopeless anymore. "Can *you* do something about this?"

"Me, personally?"

"Well, since you're the only one I seem to be talking to right now..."

"Other than helping you in your decision about what must be done, I'm afraid I must remain in the background."

"You mean you can't help me at all?"

"I can help make you aware of what your options might be..."

"In other words, you can't just wave your hand and get me back to the real world?"

He grinned. "My boy, I'm afraid things like that just aren't done. Not even in a world such as this one."

"But you made these *chairs* appear like magic..."

"This situation requires much more magic than making two chairs appear. My powers are limited. They have increased considerably over the centuries, of course, but as I just said, they are limited."

"How limited?"

"As I've told you, I am not the Almighty... Only he can work such a miracle."

"Can't you ask him to—"

He smiled sheepishly and shook his head.

"Then I'm stuck here."

"I hardly think so."

"I'm open to suggestions."

He nodded. "All right. Let's hear them."

"I was hoping *you'd* be the one to make them." I was getting more and more frustrated.

"I will—in due time."

"And when will that be?"

"When you tell me everything you know about this problem."

"I thought I did."

"Everything?"

He apparently thought I could be holding something back. Since I was pretty sure I'd told him everything, I sensed my mind rapidly approaching freeze mode. To make things even worse, portions of the meadow leading up the slope just beyond us became clearer. I sat tensely, feeling the panic building up again. A field of clover appeared where I'd seen only a few white fuzzy dots moments earlier. Some of the flowers growing wild turned brighter and more distinct. This place was steadily transforming into breathtaking mode, and I soon found that despite my dilemma, I wanted to stay and wait to view the splendor.

Then I remembered what Arthur had just told me about my spirit forming an attachment.

Suddenly frightened, I struggled to think of something I *hadn't* told him. But before I could get my brain working again, he sat back and said, "Tell me about this man's girlfriend."

"I thought I did."

"You told me you thought it was this young lady who enabled you and her boyfriend to switch spirits."

"We were having sex when this all happened."

Arthur sighed then nodded. "Something like that would definitely make you more vulnerable."

"Would that be because she had my complete attention?"

"In such a situation, distractions would be minimal. But let's move forward. Tell me more about this young lady. She could quite possibly be the key to all this."

"Izzy's her name, and she's a very spiritual girl. She's studied all sorts of religions and philosophies all her life. According to what she told me, she's an empath. I think it was her special sensitivity that told her Danny was keeping close to me. Before I'd met her, I had no idea that his spirit was right there. Everything changed the moment we met."

"How?"

"She suspected something was going on with Danny, and when I first met her, she gave me one of those looks and asked who I really was."

"What sort of look?"

"That look a female gives a guy that tells him she can actually see inside his head."

He smiled but didn't reply.

"I hope you can understand what I'm trying to say."

He nodded. "That sounds reasonable. Many sensitives can sense the thoughts and emotions of others. They also possess the ability to recognize different levels of consciousness. Their keen receptive qualities make it much easier for them to connect between worlds, to communicate with spirits that have passed over or are about to. You might consider going through her to see if you can get back."

"I doubt if she'll even respond to me right now."

"You said she's an empath, correct?"

"Yes…"

"If she is indeed a true empath, she will be the one you should choose to help you through this."

"Why do you say that?"

"Empaths will not permit themselves to cause torment or negativity for others. Negativity overwhelms them, causing severe depression. A true empath can experience another person's feelings. If this young lady is genuine, she will not permit your situation to continue. It will cause her more anguish than she'll be able to tolerate."

"Then she might be hurting over this?"

"Probably more than you can ever know."

I remembered the conversation between Izzy and Danny while I was standing on top of the hill. Arthur was right; she was indeed having trouble processing what happened.

But could I ask her to intervene without making her suffer even more in the process?

"She's really a sweet girl," I said. "I wouldn't want to subject her to any more of this than I already have."

"You must try. She could be your only chance of getting back."

"Even if she does respond, her boyfriend might object."

"Of course he will. But if you handle this correctly, he won't be aware of what you're doing."

"Then you think my one chance is to try communicating with Izzy?"

"At this stage, you might not have any other option."

"What if I can't persuade her to help me? She's got her boyfriend back. They've been in love with each other for years. Do you really think she'd do anything that might turn this around?"

"First of all, she won't want you to endure any anguish—especially something she has personally caused, either directly or indirectly. Secondly, her boyfriend might be turn out to be helpful in this as well."

"How?"

"Actually, he might not be the same person he was when he left his body."

"Whaddya mean?"

"He already left his body and came here. It was his time. And although his death was an accident, he was supposed to come here when he did. But since he returned to the land of the living when his spirit was to remain here, he won't be the same. The spirit never remains unaffected once it is brought back from another world. Once it has bonded with where its passing has taken place, it is irreversibly changed."

The reality of all this sliced into me. "What about me? Are you saying—"

"It will be different with you."

"How?"

"You haven't actually left your body."

"But I have—haven't I?"

"Not through actual death. The process was compromised."

"I'll take your word for it, but that still doesn't mean I'll be able to convince Izzy to help me do this."

"How serious are you about getting back?"

"Damned serious."

Arthur shrugged. "Then do it."

"And if it doesn't work?"

"Then you're stuck here."

"Forever?"

He nodded.

My feelings of misery and disappointment quickly returned. "I can't mess this up, can I? I have to get it right, and I've got to do it on the first try."

He smiled. "I think you'll do just fine."

"How do you know?"

"Call it intuition."

"You wouldn't want to help me with this, would you? Just to move it along a little faster?"

He winked. "Actually, I won't be *too* far away..."

"Really?"

"I did say I go where I'm needed, didn't I?"

My heart lifted. "How far away will you be?"

"Don't worry. I'll help you out when you need it."

"If that's the case, you'd better stay right here by my side."

He laughed. "Like I said, you'll do just fine. Have faith." Then he stood.

I got up. He reached out and rested his right hand on my shoulder. A strange flush of warmth flowed down my limbs and back, and I felt oddly rejuvenated.

"Just remember," he said. "She'll be much more receptive to this than you might think."

"Because she's an empath?"

"That, and because of other things."

I decided not to dwell on that right now. "Thank you, Arthur."

He smiled. "You're welcome. And if things go as well as I think they will, I'll see you in forty-two years, seven months and twenty-two days."

"I certainly hope so." I held out my hand. He extended his own. When our hands met, more warmth emanated from him, this time shimmering up my arm. I closed my eyes and bathed myself in the sensation.

A moment later, when I opened my eyes, he was gone.

The warmth from his hand remained in my palm.

Chapter 28

Nervous about what had to be done, I sat down in the grass.

Since Arthur had disappeared, his chairs had vanished with him. The grass was quite comfortable, so I didn't really mind. It was like sitting on a soft cushion.

That same moment, the shimmering glitter of the sun's reflection became more vivid above the snow-capped mountains. I began wondering what this beautiful place would look like beyond the forest…and who I would find here…and when I'd see the horses and the dogs—

You'll eventually lose all desire to leave…

Arthur's words slammed into me once again. I wasn't dead. I didn't belong here—at least, not yet. I had forty-two more years of life ahead of me and didn't plan on wasting any of it. I'd spent more than half my life working to achieve the goals that had made me successful. People depended on me. I had to concentrate on what had to be done.

I took a few deep breaths to calm myself. Then I thought of Izzy. I knew she loved Danny, but I also knew she was conscientious and honest, and felt badly for what happened. Her conversation with Danny clearly suggested that she knew this exchange of spirits just wasn't right. Arthur substantiated this when he'd told me about her character.

Feeling somewhat more confident, I closed my eyes and tried hard to project her image into my mind. Once the image was as clear as I could make it, I pushed my mental voice toward her. "Izzy?"

Nothing.

"Izzy? Can you hear me?"

This time, her image brightened, becoming more recognizable, and I sensed that I'd somehow been able to shift my spirit closer to her aura. I wondered, briefly, if this was Arthur's doing, but told myself it wasn't important—at least not now. I forced myself to concentrate on what truly *was* important.

Moments later, I heard her harsh whisper. "Who's this?"

"This is Brad, Izzy. Brad Ellis. Do you remember me?"

A gasp. "Brad? Of *course* I remember you! My God! Where *are* you?"

"I'm where Danny used to be. Listen. I need you to—"

"You're *dead*?"

"I'm trapped where Danny was when he died. Can you possibly understand what's going on?"

"I…had a feeling that's what happened. I'm *so* very sorry…"

"Izzy, listen to me. I know you love Danny, but none of this is right. We've got to somehow undo what happened."

Silence.

I could tell she didn't want to discuss this with me, but I had to keep on trying. She was my only chance to get back. "Izzy, please *talk* to me!"

Silence.

"Izzy? If you're still there, I need you to—"

"I know."

I froze. Had she said what I thought she'd said? Or had she said, *No*? My heart thumped and I felt myself going numb, but I had to proceed. "Izzy...what did you just say?"

"He's not the same, Brad. Danny...he's different, somehow. He doesn't...it seems almost like...like...he's *cruel* now. He was never *cruel* before. He always was a little arrogant, but all the musicians I've ever known are that way. But this is different, and he's scaring me. Something happened to him while he was where you are now—or maybe it happened when he came back. I don't know if this change in him came out because he passed or what, but he's not...Brad, he's just not Danny anymore!"

"Izzy, I think I know what happened, and the only thing that'll fix it is if things return to how they were before."

"You mean...Danny has to die again?"

"He's already dead, Izzy. He's just using my body right now, but his spirit belongs here, where I am right now."

"I think I understand, but I honestly don't know if we can do anything about this."

"Why not?"

"Danny definitely won't cooperate with any of it."

"I figured that one out myself. We've got to work this some other way."

"He's having too much fun, and tonight he's going over to where the band hangs out. It's a two-car garage just off Oak Ridge Road they bought a couple of years ago. They have it set up with furniture and even a small kitchen."

"Do they know what's happened?"

"He wants to show up and surprise them."

"They'll be surprised, all right."

"Brad, tell me what you want me to do. I know this shouldn't have happened, and it's…well, very wrong, but I'd really like to fix it. I was grieving for him when I lost him, but now I'm grieving for him again even though he's back. Everything's so…so *crazy* right now…"

"What's he been doing since he came back?"

A deep sigh. "He's acting really wild. It's almost like he was when he was eighteen, gigging in clubs. He wants sex all the time now, and when we're not having sex, he's drinking and eating and driving around, looking for coke. He can't score from his regular guys because he's trapped in your body and none of his contacts recognize him. This drives him crazy, so he's going to all the bad places in Orlando to score from sleazeballs who'll sell bad stuff to anyone. He told me he was almost stabbed last night. Brad, this is horrible!"

I shivered with rage. We had to fix this quickly, or her idiot boyfriend would get me stabbed or worse before I could get my body back. But I couldn't let this beat me. I had to concentrate on

234

what had to be done. Izzy and I had to pool our efforts to somehow reverse this fiasco.

"Izzy, I know he told you what happened that night. The night he died."

A pause. "Brad, I know you were the one...who killed him."

I felt a sharp tug where my heart should have been. "Izzy, I'm so very, *very* sorry... I wish...I really wish—"

"It wasn't your fault. I know that now. If it hadn't been you, it would've been someone else. But that's not important now. We've got to—"

Silence.

"Izzy?"

"Danny's coming back."

"Izzy, *please* don't break contact with me..."

"I'll make sure I keep you with me. Just keep thinking of me, and we'll both figure out a way to fix this."

"Thanks."

***

"Baby, why aren't you gettin' ready?" Danny's voice grew louder as he approached Izzy. "I'm leavin' in half an hour."

"Danny, where have you been?"

"I had to score some blow. I thought you knew that."

"*Danny!*"

"I never thought I'd hate this guy Ellis, but he must've been a real dork. Everyone I tried scorin' with pegged me as a damn Narc."

"You didn't really expect them to deal with you, did you? They don't *know* you anymore. There's no reason why they should. That's one of the disadvantages of looking different. Face it, Danny—you're a different person now…"

"I figured on somethin' like that. That's why I tried hittin' Norville first. Norville will sell to anyone. I even offered the bastard an extra twenty, but he just told me to get bent and walked away. It was like…like he was afraid of me."

"Danny, it's the vibes you're giving off. Others can feel them, you know."

"That shithead Norville couldn't feel his own dick without grabbin' it first. Baby, you've been studyin' that spiritual shit much too long. It's givin' you all sorts of crazy ideas."

"I can feel them, too, Danny."

"Feel what, baby?"

"Your vibes. They're different. *You're* different. It's like…like there are actually two of you, and the vibes you're giving off…well, they're mixing well with Brad's, and—"

"You're getting' weird on me again, baby."

"Danny, please *listen* to me!"

"It's got nothin' to do with vibes, baby. It's Ellis. They see Ellis—not me. Don't put anything more complicated into it. These are dealers I'm tryin' to hit on—not brain surgeons. They don't know from vibes, baby."

Izzy didn't reply.

"I also tried Santos. You know him. He'd sell his sister for a price."

"Did he sell you any coke?"

"Bastard walked away, too. This Ellis dude…he must've had somethin' wrong with him. Makes ya wonder how he was rich enough to afford that ride of his…and that pad in Winter Park…"

"Danny, we've got to talk about this."

"About what?"

"About your coming back. It's not right. You should know that by now."

"Because a couple of shitheads refused to sell me blow? Gimme another day or two. I'll find someone who likes the color of Ellis' money. Money's money. No one cares about vibes when ya wave a batch of greenbacks in their faces."

"Danny, this is really bothering me. I don't see you, I see Brad—"

"Baby, I already told ya, you'll get used to this guy's looks. He ain't *that* bad-lookin', is he?"

"It's not his looks I'm concerned about, Danny!"

"What's the problem, then?"

"You honestly can't see it, can you?"

"See what, baby? You're talkin' in riddles again."

"If you can't see it, that's the problem."

"Those ideas of yours—"

"They're not just ideas, Danny…"

"What *is* all this, then?"

A deep sigh. "You're not *you* anymore!"

"There's a good reason for that, and you know it."

"I know what's happened, and I feel horrible about it."

"You feel horrible about bringing me back?"

Silence.

"Baby, *talk* to me!"

"Danny, none of this is right. You're back, but you're not *you* anymore. Otherwise, I could get used to you looking like Brad... But it isn't like that. You've come back, but it's not really you. You're just not the same!"

"Baby, at least I came back. And just in case you haven't figured it out yet, let me let ya in on a little secret: it wasn't easy."

"I know. Believe me. I got the call from the police. I know what happened. I knew the moment they gave me your gig bag."

"Aren't you glad I'm back, baby?"

Silence.

"Baby?"

"Danny, you shouldn't *be* back!"

"But I *am*, dammit! What the fuck's wrong? I thought you'd *want* me back!"

"Danny..."

"What's the damn problem, baby?"

"Like I said, this isn't right. You shouldn't be here. It's against...it's against *everything*. Brad should be here, and you should—"

"Are you saying you'd rather have Ellis here than me?"

"I'm saying this just isn't right. It's totally against God and logic and all the laws of the Universe. There's got to be an order to everything,

238

or nothing works right. This—your coming back from wherever you were—it's just not natural. This has to be why you're not the same...why you're so angry...why you're not really *you* anymore."

"It doesn't matter that it's against God and all those stupid fuckin' laws, baby. It happened, and don't tell me you didn't want me to come back. Don't you remember how you were moanin' and callin' for me when you were makin' it with Ellis?"

"I didn't know what I was doing, Danny! I was...sort of...well, in a trance. I kept hearing you...seeing you...feeling you...and the more I called for you, the closer you felt to me. I had no idea that I'd actually be able to bring you back!"

"Well, that spiritual mumbo-jumbo you've been studyin' all these years finally paid off. I'm back, and I intend to stay here as long as I can."

"Danny...you just can't *do* this... It isn't *you!*"

"What's wrong, baby? What's got your panties in a wad?"

Silence.

"Baby?"

"Danny, you're *dead*. I love you with all my heart, but you really should be *dead*!"

Silence.

"Danny, where are you going?"

"You know where I'm goin'."

"We need to talk about this!"

"This is all that I'm gonna say right now, so take it or leave it. I'm gonna get cleaned up to get ready to drive over to Oak Ridge. The guys are there, and they're prob'ly tryin' to figure out what the hell they're gonna do without me. You know what this town's like. There's not a horn player in Central Florida I couldn't blow rings around in my sleep. Even Disney doesn't have a player as good as me. Those boys are in a pickle. I'm gonna bail their asses out and they're really gonna freak!"

"You actually think you can just go on over there and tell them you really didn't die? That this is you in someone else's body?"

A chuckle. "Baby, what the hell do ya take me for? If I do that, they'll all run for the hills. Or they'll just tell me to fuck myself and toss me out on my ear. No, I've got my own trump card. I'm takin' Bessie with me. She's all I'll need."

"Your horn. You're taking your horn, and you think that'll fix everything."

"Yeah. I'm takin' my horn. Believe me, what comes outa her will fix everything."

"But they saw you the other day. Actually, they saw Brad, and he didn't mention anything about playing. In fact, he said he didn't play at all. It was the truth. He's not a musician. Don't you think your friends will be suspicious when he shows up with your horn and can suddenly play just as well as you could?"

"Stay with me here, okay? And try a little harder to keep up. I bring in Bessie and tell the guys I just went to Raymond's the other night to offer them my condolences. I'm a damn good horn player, but I didn't wanna show off while they were grievin', especially with a dead guy's horn, so I just left. I decided to wait a few days, then drive on over

240

and tell 'em I'm lookin' for a band. They're desperate, so they'll wanna hear me. I take Bessie out of the gig bag, play her, and *voila*! The band has their star horn player again!"

"You honestly think that'll work?"

"Of course it'll work. You heard me play yesterday, didn't you?"

"Yes…"

"How'd I sound?"

"You sounded fantastic."

"Of course I did. I'm still me—in spite of everything you're tryin' to unload on me. Now…you wanna come with me? Then come with me. You don't wanna come? Then stay here and enjoy this freaky moment you seem to be havin'. I have more important things to do."

"Danny?"

Silence.

Chapter 29

Just moments later, I heard Izzy's voice again.

She sounded like she'd been crying. "I'm really sorry, Brad. I couldn't...I just couldn't make him understand!"

"I heard every word, Izzy. I want to thank you for trying."

"I don't know what else I can do. *Sniff*. He seems dead-set on going back to the band...*sniff*...and picking up where he left off."

"I heard that, too."

"When he's like this, no one can talk to him. He's just like he was when he was drinking and doing coke. He had it in his head that he was going to do what he wanted and didn't care what anyone else thought. But now it's much worse. He's...so *angry*..."

"I know. I could hear it in his voice."

"I just don't know what else I can do. Do you have any ideas?"

"I wish I did..."

"I don't *want* to go to Oak Ridge with him. I just...I've got this feeling..."

"Tell me about it."

"I can't put it into words. I just feel strongly that something bad will happen if he goes there and tries to convince them he's not really dead."

You need to go with her...

I had no idea where that thought came from. It sounded as if it had come right out of the blue. I

242

wondered if it was my subconscious communicating with me again, just as it was doing right after the accident with Danny.

But this felt different. This thought felt lighter, warmer, optimistic…

Arthur? Was that you?

Nothing.

Arthur?

It didn't matter, did it? Arthur's touch, his reassuring words and his smile—they all suggested that whatever he told me would be the right thing to do.

I'll help you when you need it…

I suddenly felt more confident than ever before.

"Izzy, you need to go with him."

"I don't know… If something bad is gonna happen, I really don't want to be there. You understand, don't you?"

"Trust me. You need to go with him, and you need to take me with you."

"Do you have…some sort of an idea…what to do?"

"I just feel that we've got to go there and be with him."

"Are you sure? I mean, really and truly *sure*?"

"Yes."

A pause. "Brad, tell me about where you are."

"Izzy, we really can't get into this right now. Maybe later, if things turn out all right."

"You don't know how deeply I feel about this stuff. I've gone all my life wondering about the afterlife, and now here you are, right there, and you're in my head—which means the afterlife is also in my head. I need to feel it, sense it, experience it. Can't you at least tell me a little about it?"

"All I can say right now is that it's—"

"Darn it… Danny's coming back. What do I do now?"

"Act yourself, and don't say anything that'll make him suspicious. Got it?"

"Got it. I just hope you're right about all this."

"I am. And don't forget, I'm right here. If my instinct is on the mark, this might turn out well for both of us."

"Why the hell aren't you getting ready?" Danny sounded even angrier than before.

"Just a sec, Danny… I just need to brush my hair and put on some fresh eye shadow."

"Get a move on. I wanna get there before this century ends."

"Yes, Danny…"

***

While Izzy went to get ready, I thought about what I could do once Danny got together with his friends.

Since hearing his conversation with Izzy, I knew what he planned to do and realized that he might actually be able to pull it off. Even so, I was in a much better position than I was before. At least I felt better, knowing Izzy was on my side.

As I thought about all this, something caught my attention. The light-blue haze that had puzzled me before had become crystal clear, turning into a sparkling pond. Just beyond it, the white blurred form rose vertically, and I could hear the distinctive roar of a waterfall. I knew that if this continued, the waterfall would eventually reveal itself vividly to me. I found that I wanted it to happen quickly so I could continue sitting here and appreciate its beauty—

Your spirit is already forming an attachment to this world.

It will soon become entranced, and you'll eventually lose all desire to leave.

Once again, Arthur's words forced me to turn away from the beauty unfolding before me and focus on my problem. What seemed like just a minute or so later, I thought I heard Izzy and Danny getting into a car. I immediately shifted my attention back to business, closed my eyes and focused.

"Nice ride, eh, baby?"

"Yes, Danny…"

"You know this is the same ride that killed me, don'tcha?"

A pause. As I concentrated on situating myself more firmly into her aura, I could feel the tension building up inside her.

"I really wish you hadn't told me that," she whispered.

"No problem, doll. Things are different now. Revenge can be really sweet."

Izzy didn't reply. The tension growing in her turned hot.

"As I said before, that Ellis dude must've been worth some serious cash. This car goes for between sixty and eighty K. I really need to go back to that dude's pad and check it out better. When I was there last night, I found a coupla K in a big jar under the end table in his bedroom. You know damn well that a guy like him has got to have helluva stash somewhere else. Once I get back with the band and we start bookin' gigs again, I'm gonna make a trip to his bank and make a big withdrawal."

It took all my self-control to remain silent.

"Danny, you really need to think about what you're doing." The tension within her grew even hotter.

"Baby, I'm gettin' sick and tired of this nagging. You know how I hate that shit. That's what always turned me on so much about you. You weren't like those other babes who brought a guy down once she got hold of his 'nads. That's why I never wanted to hang out with anyone else. I always liked that you were different and let me be myself. You've been like that since we first met. You always were one prime lady." He chuckled. "Those nice little titties of yours didn't hurt, either."

"Oh, Danny…"

I felt the warm flash of her embarrassment even before she'd spoken.

"What's wrong? It's not like someone can hear us, is it?"

She just sighed.

"The thing is, you *never* nagged—not even when those bitches were comin' onto me once we started playin' Disney. I really appreciated that, baby. That's what's bummin' me out right now. Why the hell are ya so damn uptight lately?"

Another sigh. "Because you shouldn't *be* here, Danny…"

Silence.

"Is there somethin' you're not tellin' me, baby?"

No reply.

"If you're tryin' to tell me that you were gettin' off on that Ellis dude—"

"It isn't that at all…"

"I didn't like him comin' on to ya like he did, if ya wanna know the truth. And I sure didn't like him pawin' all over ya…but it was the only way I knew to get back. I don't know what ya did or how ya did it, but it worked, and I'm really glad everything came out all right."

"But it *didn't*, Danny…"

"Whaddya mean? I'm back, right?"

"Yes. You're back."

"Then what didn't come out right?"

"The fact that you're back…"

Silence.

"One day you're gonna have to explain that to me, baby."

"I can't."

"Why the hell not?"

"No matter what I say, you just wouldn't understand."

"How do ya know?"

247

"I've been telling you what's wrong for the last couple of days, but you, obviously haven't heard a word I've said."

"I've heard everything you've said."

"What have I said?"

"You're bummed out because we did somethin' wrong—somethin' against the laws of the fuckin' Universe. Somethin' that shouldn't have happened. Isn't that about right?"

"Yes, Danny. That's absolutely right."

"Far out. I got it. Still think I don't understand?"

"Yes, Danny. I really and truly think you don't understand."

"Why the hell do the hottest chicks always have to be the most fucked up in the head?"

"I don't know about anyone else, but I do know what's right and what's wrong. Believe me—this just isn't right!"

"Listen, baby… We're gonna be there in just a coupla minutes. Try really hard not to embarrass me with this stupid Pollyanna attitude of yours in front of Bill and the guys, okay? It's gonna be a real bitch anyway, gettin' back with them. I don't want you around to mess with their minds."

"Why *do* you want me around, Danny?"

He chuckled. "I want you to see their jaws drop to the fuckin' floor when they hear me play again—why else?"

Chapter 30

The barking of a dog far off in the distance broke my concentration.

Then I heard the far-off thundering sound of a galloping horse. I turned. The waterfall had become much clearer.

This place was quickly unfolding before my eyes. I had to literally struggle to keep from gazing at it. I reminded myself once again that no matter how beautiful it was, I didn't belong here. If my life went as scheduled, I'd return forty-two years from now. Then I could sit here forever and bathe myself in the majestic beauty of this Eden.

But now I had to focus on getting back to my present world. I closed my eyes and once again began focusing.

As I settled back into the tense darkness of Izzy's spirit, I realized Danny was parking my car. The two of them had been silent for quite a while, but the tension—as well as the hurt—emanating from Izzy hadn't diminished.

I'll do my best to help you, I told her.

Although she didn't reply, I could feel the tension inside her easing up a little.

Danny said, "Remember what I told ya. Don't embarrass me or say anything stupid. You know how important this is to me. If you do anything to screw it up, I'm liable to start lookin' for someone else. And ya know damn well that I can prob'ly find one in no time at all. A babe called that Ellis dude's phone, said her name was Vera, and damn, she sounded hot. She wanted to come right over, said somethin' about polishin' off that bubbly in the fridge. But I had other things on my mind and told her I'd take a rain check. Just think about shit like that before ya start naggin' me again."

I wanted to strangle the bastard.

"Get it, baby?" he asked.

"I get it." The tension in her had increased dramatically.

The car doors opened and slammed shut, and soon they were walking up the walk. I heard one of them—Danny, no doubt—opening a creaky door.

Concentrate…get closer to Izzy…

I soon entered the bright warmth of Izzy's aura. I could tell she sensed what I was doing. She stopped walking and took a deep breath.

It's only me, I whispered at her.

She nodded. *I'm glad you're here. I'm frightened.*

No need to be. We'll just take this one step at a time.

"Somethin' wrong?" Danny asked.

"Whatever would make you think that?" she asked flatly.

"Ya look…well, spacey…"

"I'm fine."

"You sure?"

"I said I'm okay…"

"Then get with the program."

The brightness of Izzy's aura surrounded me. I could feel her warmth shimmering down my limbs.

Seconds later, the brightness thinned and then cleared, and through her eyes I was soon able to watch as we followed Danny into the garage, where his three friends sat at a metal folding table, sharing a joint and drinking beer. Six cans of beer, two tin ashtrays littered with butts, a big glass bowl of beer nuts and two bags of Ruffles and Doritos cluttered the table.

Danny walked right in and stood there, watching them. Izzy and I stayed about five feet behind Danny.

The three men turned our way and stared.

Ten seconds of silence.

Bill put his beer can on the table and squinted. "You're the dude came over to the club last week."

"I guess you could say that."

"Whaddya doin' with Danny's axe?" Chopper was staring at the gig bag Danny cradled in the crook of my arm.

Danny shrugged. "I figured that since that Danny dude got dusted, you boys would need a good horn player, so I brought it along with me."

Nick sat up and dropped the tiny stub of his blunt in the ashtray in front of him. He pushed out a slender stream of gray smoke. "How'd *you* get it?"

"Izzy gave it to me."

Both Chopper and Bill shook their heads. I could see the skepticism in their faces. Bill slowly stood. His stern expression suggested that he wasn't buying any of this. "Izzy wouldn't turn over Danny's axe to just any dude."

"What's goin' on, Izzy?" Chopper asked.

The tension quickly increased in Izzy's spirit. Her aura had darkened; some cold drifted through us.

You're going to be okay, I told her. *Just relax. I'm pretty sure I've got this covered.*

She took a deep breath. Her aura grew somewhat lighter. "I think you'd better listen to what he's got to say."

"You tellin' us you *play*?" Bill moved closer.

Danny shrugged. "Why else would I be luggin' this gig bag all over town with me?"

Bill took another step toward Danny. "Why didn't ya mention this at the club?"

"You guys were in a bad way, hearin' about Danny and all."

"That's right." Nick picked up a beer nut and sucked thoughtfully on it. "You came over to console us in our grief," he said flatly.

"You could say that," Danny said.

"We've got a regular Mother Teresa watchin' out for us now," Nick added, grinning.

The others chuckled.

Danny sighed. "Listen here, dammit. I didn't come here just so you dudes could load a bunch of shit on me..."

"Why *did* ya show, then?" Bill asked.

"I was bein' considerate the other night. You dudes had a lot on your plate."

Chopper and Nick both grinned.

"Considerate how?" Bill asked.

"I didn't wanna just come over and say, hey dudes, don't worry. I'm a motherfucker on the horn,

252

too, so if ya wanna keep your gigs, I got your backs."

Chopper and Nick got up and walked over. Chopper said, "Then you're tellin' us you *can* actually play?"

"Like I just said...why else would I be luggin' this horn around?"

"He's holdin' it just like Danny used to," Nick said softly.

Bill tilted his head. "Noticed that too, eh?"

Chopper said, "Dude, ya just don't sound like ya did at the club."

Bill nodded. "Noticed *that*, too..."

"How do I sound?" Danny asked.

"Cocky," Bill said. "It's like you're totin' around a pair of some heavy-duty 'nads."

"Somethin's off," Nick said, frowning. "Somethin's *way* the hell off..."

"What the fuck's goin' on, Izzy?" Bill asked.

She tensed up again. Her aura grew darker and began to cool.

Tell them to listen to what he's got to say, I prompted her.

"You really need to listen to him," she said softly.

Bill continued staring at her. So did the others.

"You guys ready for a real kick in the ass?" Danny said.

Silence.

After about twenty seconds, Bill said, "Yeah." He crossed his lean, hairy forearms in front of him.

"Lately my fuckin' ass has been in the mood for a real kick. So start kickin'."

"Let's hear what you got," Chopper said with a sneer.

"Thought you'd never ask." Danny took the gig bag over to the beat-up sofa, set it down on the cushion, unzipped it and gently removed the horn from its resting place.

I could feel Izzy tensing up again.

***

Concentrate even more, the voice inside me said, and this time I could tell it was Arthur. His voice convinced me he'd been with me all along, and I knew right then that I was going to accomplish what had to be done.

Focus on Danny Glen, the voice continued, and concentrate on moving closer and closer to your physical presence... Use the young lady's aura as light to help you move forward. Then drift freely, until you've entered your physical body again. Once you've returned home, remain as unnoticeable as you possibly can. Do this gently and quietly. If you do it properly, the spirit who stole your body will not be able to suspect your return...

Concentrate on my essence, I told Izzy. *Concentrate on sending me as close to my physical body as you can...and while you're doing it, don't think of Danny at all. Focus only on me and make believe that the man standing in front of you is actually me—not Danny. Can you do this?*

I think so...

254

I immediately sensed her essence brightening as it focused on the figure in front of us, moving closer, until I began feeling my own essence flowing through Izzy. Her spirit grew much warmer, and she shuddered.

It's all right, I told her, and she relaxed.

Although Danny was only a few feet away, my essence felt much closer. The moment I sensed my spirit meshing with hers, I drifted forward and soon felt my soul slipping into my own body, as if I was positioning myself behind the wheel of my car.

For a moment I thought I might have somehow given myself away. Danny stiffened slightly, pausing just as he took his trumpet out of the bag.

"Somethin' wrong?" Bill asked.

I forced myself to relax, to remain quiet and invisible…and, by concentrating on complete darkness, I sensed his spirit relaxing as well.

"Not a damn thing." Danny turned and glanced at Izzy. I wanted to tell her to empty her mind of all thoughts and emotions. I didn't need to. She knew what was going on. She stood there in silence, her eyes in his direction, but I could tell she wasn't looking directly at him.

"Ya gonna do somethin'?" Nick asked. "You're wastin' our time."

"Hold your water." Running a hand through my hair, Danny turned back to what he was doing. While he worked the valves of his trumpet, I settled back into my warm niche and remained as invisible as possible. Danny pulled the mouthpiece from its pouch and twisted it carefully into the lead pipe of the instrument.

"Danny liked the Goz." Bill was watching us intently. His expression remained skeptical. "Ever heard of him?"

Danny was using my lips to blow into the mouthpiece. He pushed open the spit valve and blew into it again, then opened the spit valve on the third valve slide and blew a second time. He worked the valves once again for about ten seconds, this time much more vigorously. Satisfied with the action, we turned around where Bill and the others were standing, watching us. "Conrad Gozzo. Damn straight. Who the hell *hasn't* heard of that dude?" he said with a shrug.

"Ever heard of *"Trumpeter's Prayer"*?" Chopper asked. "That was Danny's favorite chart."

"I've played it a few times."

"It's a motherfucker of a chart," Bill said.

"I seem to have heard that somewhere," Danny said, chuckling softly.

"Only a handful of horn players can do it— especially in the key the Goz played it in."

"I've heard that one, too."

Nick was frowning. "No one except the Goz himself could play it as well as Danny."

"I'll give it helluva try..." Danny grinned devilishly as he brought the mouthpiece up.

"Play it even half as good as Danny did," Bill said. "If you can do that, you've got a steady gig with us."

"No problem." Then he pressed the mouthpiece to my lips and took a deep breath.

***

The moment I watched the horn rise in front of my face, a strange darkness came from out of nowhere and fell over me.

Warmth surrounded me, and I began to feel a slight tingling in my hands...and in my arms...and then everything else. Blackness enveloped me and I soon felt as if I'd just appeared in the room. My initial reaction was to panic, but some bizarre sensation inside me made me realize everything would turn out all right and that the darkness would soon lift.

Everything will be all right, Arthur's soft, reassuring voice said. *Focus, and take over the moment he begins to play.*

Once the cold brass mouthpiece pressed tightly against my lips, I felt myself taking a deep breath to begin the song.

Now forget about Danny Glen and take control of your body again, Arthur said.

Just like that? I asked, suddenly confused.

Just like that, Arthur replied.

An instant later, just as I began to fully understand what Arthur had just told me, Danny and I blew into the mouthpiece.

A sound like the bellowing of an enraged elephant thundered from the glistening bell of the horn.

Chapter 31

Laughter reverberated off the concrete walls.

The three men sat at the table, laughing hysterically. Nick had just finished a swig of beer and bent forward, hacking away. Bill finished laughing and began to choke. Behind me, Izzy was covering her mouth with her hands. Tears filled her eyes.

Damn...what the fuck happened? Danny's thoughts were so loud that they reverberated in my head. *Damn mouthpiece must be clogged!*

With Danny's help, I lowered the horn, removed the mouthpiece and brought it to my lips. I blew into it—just as he wished. The air went through freely, so we screwed it back on and raised the horn once again. I felt him tensing my arms. Then, taking a deep breath, I let him pull in a huge gulp of air. He then mashed the mouthpiece against my lips and I forced a second batch of repulsive, ear-splitting air roaring through the horn.

Once again, the three men howled laughter. Chopper groaned, bent forward in his chair and covered his face with both hands. Nick rubbed his ears vigorously, forced his eyes closed and shook his head. Bill had stopped laughing and sat bolt upright, watching me as if he was looking at something he'd never seen before.

As I lowered the horn, I could feel Danny studying it while struggling to understand what had gone wrong. My heart was pounding, but I could tell it was due to the panic enveloping him. A whirlwind of emotions flowed all around us. His aura darkened and grew cold, with flashes of heat sputtering from the back of my neck.

A moment later, I felt him stiffen inside me. His aura instantly grew darker.

You bastard, he muttered, and another splash of heat crept down my back. *You're there, aren'tcha? You found a way to come back!*

Yes, Danny, I'm right here.

How the fuck did ya get back? Did Izzy help ya?

That doesn't matter, does it? I'm back—just like you.

You bastard!

Did you really expect me to just stay there and let you live the rest of my life?

I coulda got my career back! Why the hell did ya do it? What the fuck have ya done?

What do you think? I replied. *I reclaimed my body.*

Another splash of heat slid down my spine. *You can't do this, you asshole! You can't fuckin' do this to me!*

Sorry, Danny, it's already done...

Damn you...damn you...damn—

Sorry, but it had to be done. You know that. What you did—well, it was against every single law of Nature.

Fuck Nature! You made me humiliate myself! In front of my friends!

They'll think it's me, so you don't have to worry about your reputation—

Fuck! You can't do this! I had a chance here!

You gave me no choice.

I wanted another chance! I deserved another chance! I was a damn good player! I coulda been one of the best, dammit! We were gonna cut a single in a month or so. Bill's got this friend, works in one of the sound studios at Disney—

Go away, Danny. Go back where you belong.

I didn't... belong there, dammit! You put me there!

I could feel his voice growing softer as his spirit slowly drifted away. The weight of his trumpet began to grow in my arms.

I know I did, and I'm sorry...but I can't go back and change it...and neither can you...

You can't...this sucks...this really sucks...I can't...goddammit...Izzy? Can ya hear me, baby? Tell this asshole—

She won't help you, Danny...

What did ya do to her, you bastard? She's right here...why can't she—

She knows where you belong, Danny...

Damn you...damn both of you...it isn't fair...

It's where you belong now, Danny. You can play your horn there forever...

Not fair...not—

Then he was gone.

I took in a deep gulp of genuine relief. Then I looked down at myself. My shoes. My pants. My shirt. Everything was mine again—especially my body. I wanted to cry. If there hadn't been three strange guys sitting over there, watching me, I would have let myself go.

Then I got control of myself and turned.

Izzy was standing just a few feet away, watching me, the tears staining her cheeks, her mascara running. She reached out and placed a tiny hand on my wrist. "B-Brad?" she asked hesitantly, in a whisper.

I smiled. "It's me again."

She swallowed. "D-Danny?"

"He's gone, Izzy. I'm sorry…I really and truly am."

She squeezed my wrist. Another tear drifted down her cheek. "I know I must sound horrible for saying this, but—"

"I know how you feel."

As we stared into each other's eyes, I felt genuine affection for this sweet young woman. I sensed that it was the same warmth I'd experienced when Izzy had visited me in my condo. Was it possible I was falling in love with this special lady? The connection I shared with her when I gazed into those beautiful brown eyes was unmistakable, and I could feel the electricity growing between us as—

Someone coughed behind me.

Bill had come over. He was watching both of us and looked angry. "What the fuck was *that* all about, dude?"

My first instinct was to turn around and get out of there as quickly as possible. But I knew that wouldn't be wise or practical. I'd be leaving Izzy behind, and she'd have to come up with something to explain all this.

"No offense," Bill added, "but you can't play a lick, can ya?"

I just shrugged. Then I turned around and opened the gig bag. "I used to play," I lied. "It was a long time ago, and I was actually pretty good." I carefully replaced the horn in the bag, zipped it shut and picked it up. Then I turned to face them. "I haven't played in years, but I thought I could at least sound a little better than...well..." I shrugged.

Bill scowled. He kept shaking his head. "You were wrong, dude. Dead wrong."

"I guess so. Sorry about that."

"When was the last time you actually played?"

I sighed. "In high school."

He blinked. "How long ago was that?"

"Not quite twenty years."

Nick and Chopper chuckled.

"You haven't played in *twenty years*?" Bill's dark eyes filled the sockets. "You didn't even try to get your chops back before ya came here? And you were gonna try and play the *Goz chart*? In front of three professionals?"

I shrugged. "I guess that *was* kind of stupid of me..."

Bill groaned. "Ya *think*?"

"Changed your attitude a tad, didn't it?" Chopper asked.

"What's that?"

"You ain't nearly as cocky as you were when you first came in."

262

"Yeah. Sorry about that, too. Izzy told me you'd be ecstatic if you found another decent horn player. I really thought I could get by. I never considered that I'd lose my chops altogether."

"Ya don't use 'em, ya lose 'em, man," Nick said.

"Doesn't take long at all," Bill said.

"Stay away from the skins for a fuckin' month," Chopper said. "You'll be lucky to get in a good roll when ya get back to 'em."

I nodded.

"And ya haven't buzzed a mouthpiece in *twenty years*?" Bill obviously found this incredible.

I sighed. "I guess so..."

Bill turned and went back to the table. "Ya know of anybody who actually *can* play, let us know." He sat and picked up his beer.

"I sure will."

No one else said anything, but I could feel all three of them watching me as I left and went back outside.

I was about to get back in my car when I heard light footsteps behind me. It was Izzy, and she was frowning at me. "I could use a ride home, if you don't mind too much."

I didn't know what to say. I'd assumed she would have wanted to stay with her friends.

Her dark brows mashed together. "You forgot about me, didn't you?"

"No..."

"Then why didn't you ask me to leave with you?"

"I just thought...I figured you would have wanted to stay here with your friends."

"They're *Danny's* friends. At least, they were..."

"I'm sorry, Izzy. I guess I had things figured wrong."

She slipped into the seat beside me. I handed her the gig bag. She took it and held it against her chest directly over her heart. The tears gathered again. Once the moment passed, she sighed and rested it in her lap. Her eyes stayed on it. "He's really gone now, isn't he?"

"I'm afraid so."

She sniffed. "Danny was really a terrific guy before...well, before."

"I know."

"You two might have even become friends if he hadn't...if you—"

"If I hadn't killed him?"

She smiled and nodded.

"Life sure is funny sometimes," I said.

"Sometimes it's too much for anyone to bear," she said softly, still gazing at the gig bag.

I backed down the driveway, eased onto Oak Ridge Road, and we were soon on our way.

Chapter 32

Ten minutes later, as we followed the line of traffic through the busy intersection of Oak Ridge and South Orange Blossom Trail, I could tell something was on Izzy's mind. She hadn't said anything for the last couple of miles. She sat quite still, her hands on the gig bag in her lap as she stared straight ahead.

I was just about to ask if something was wrong when she said, "Tell me about it, Brad. Tell me about where you were."

I'd hoped she wouldn't have asked me about it so soon. I was still trying to come to grips with the experience myself. I figured I needed time to get it together before I could decide what really happened. If I hadn't had so many other things on my mind, I might have driven myself crazy just thinking about it. But now that the crisis was over and I was back in the real world, I knew I'd have to take a step back and re-evaluate everything. But at the moment, I wasn't sure if I was quite ready.

"I really want to know," she said. "I *have* to know. I need to know all about it. Everything you can tell me. Every single thing you remember." She sighed, wrapped her arms around herself and sat back in her seat. She was smiling at me. "It would be so wonderful to find out that I've been right about it all these years. You have no idea how many times I've wanted to tell all these non-believers that there really is an actual place beyond this world their spirit goes to when it leaves their body. So many people believe that once you die, that's it. Everything's over, and you become part of the earth. I know better. Energy never dies, and once you're born, you're a spirit forever. But you can't tell a non-believer anything. You've got to show them. But even then, they're skeptical. If they don't want to believe in something, they won't—no matter what they see or don't see. I figure that since you were there, you could tell me everything. And even if no one believed me, I'd know for sure, because you were there. I know for a fact that you were because Danny came back from the same place." She uncrossed her arms. "So now I'd like you to tell me everything. Every single detail, from the time Danny tricked you into going there. I really need you to."

"Now?"

"Yes. Right now. Right this second."

As I drove, my thoughts went back to when Izzy came to my condo…to the time she got up to leave, turned to face me, and the magic between us took over. I remembered the moment we were in my bed, making love. I fondly remembered that very special moment when we first kissed…and when I lay on top of her…and when we became one. And the moment she began calling out for Danny. And when the darkness came, sweeping over us…

Then the darkness cleared, and Izzy began drifting away. Soon I couldn't feel her at all. She called out for Danny, and even though I could see

266

everything, it was as if I'd been pulled away and held in a different sphere.

And when the darkness came once again, all the special moments Izzy and I had shared suddenly ended.

The instant it lifted, that strange brightness came up and whisked me away. Izzy disappeared, and I soon realized I was no longer with her. And then...

Nothing.

"Brad?"

I struggled to remember, but for some reason, I just couldn't recall what happened after the brightness had taken me away. Once it swept up, whatever happened afterward had become a giant void. Briefly I had some vague recollection of encountering some other spirit. A flash of gray—or was it white?—skittered by and vanished. I also had a strong feeling that this spirit might have helped me and could have even been responsible for sending Danny back ...

But the moment I tried grasping for more of the details, everything vanished.

"Brad, what's wrong?"

"I can't...I just can't remember."

"What can't you remember?"

I shrugged. "Anything."

She watched me closely, probably trying to decide if I was lying. "You don't remember *anything* that happened when you switched places with Danny?"

"I know it must sound absolutely incredible, but no. I really don't."

"You're sure?"

I sighed. "My mind goes blank each time I struggle to recall the details."

"What *do* you remember?"

I stopped at the next light, closed my eyes and tried to clear my head. I took a few deep breaths. For a moment I thought I remembered the darkness lifting again, but as soon as the brightness returned, my thoughts disappeared. I even thought I heard a voice telling me that I wasn't supposed to remember. Then I wondered if it was just my own consciousness intervening, possibly to spare me from some other trauma.

I opened my eyes and rubbed my temples. The light changed. We began moving again.

"Anything?" she asked.

I shook my head.

She was silent for the next few miles. I hoped I hadn't upset her. I also hoped she wouldn't think I was purposely keeping this from her. She appeared deep in thought.

"You believe me, don't you?" I asked.

"Actually, I think I understand."

"Really?"

"I honestly don't think we're supposed to know anything about it until our time comes."

"You could be absolutely right." I hadn't even considered that possibility.

"The way people are, wouldn't you agree that such a sensitive subject needs to be kept safe at all costs?"

I nodded. "People can't keep their mouths shut—even when it involves the most trivial, insignificant things. Something like this? Hell, it wouldn't be kept secret more than five seconds before going viral and then global in minutes. We both know how predictable people are when it comes to stuff like this. They'd go absolutely crazy with it. Hollywood would get wind of it and turn it into a reality show. And when the TV ministers hear about it, they'll turn it into something really disgusting. In any case, a phenomenon like this would easily be turned into something I don't even want to think about."

Izzy went silent. After some thought, she said, "You were *somewhere*, though, weren't you?"

"I'm almost certain I was."

"It wasn't a bad place, was it?"

"I honestly can't remember."

"Do you remember anything you told Danny before you…before he went back?"

It's where you belong now, Danny. You can play your horn there forever…

Had I told him that? Or was this just my mind playing tricks? Was I trying to substitute the vast emptiness in my memory banks with something positive I could tell her? Something that would enable me to save face?

"Anything at all?" she asked, sounding hopeful.

"I think I remember telling him he could play his horn there forever."

Izzy smiled. "Okay. Then at least you remember that, right?"

"But apparently nothing else."

"It's a start. If there wasn't anything there to begin with, and if you told him he could play his horn there, you wouldn't have said it, right?"

"Right…"

"You sound doubtful."

"I am."

"I truly feel that we're not supposed to know anything about it until we're actually sent there."

"The thing that's bothering me is that if it was such a great place, why was Danny so obsessed with coming back?"

"He wasn't." Izzy's expression turned grim. "It wasn't Danny's idea to come back. Not at first, anyway…"

I was impressed that she'd been able to pick up on what Danny had said to me when we had our "chat."

"When I first met you, I felt him," she said. "When I saw you again at the mall, I felt him again, but even stronger than before. You were responsible for his death and felt so badly that you couldn't let him rest in peace. You kept him so close to you that you prevented him from passing over. You kept holding him back. Don't feel badly about it. I was holding him back, too. And when you and I met, I was so overwhelmed with sensations that I really believed you were Danny. The two of us brought him back."

"Was that even possible?"

"It happened, didn't it?"

"I guess it did."

She was silent for a few moments. Then she looked at me and said, "So where do we go from here?"

That was a good question. I knew that in my own case, I had to start focusing once again on my career. Ellis & Associates had to continue, which meant my going back to work and taking the helm again. I had to complete the merger and get everything running again.

But what about Izzy? Could I consider her a part of my future? Or was she just someone I'd encountered during a very bizarre traumatic event? I had to remind myself that what we'd shared was very special, and that such an experience would forever stay with me. Although I'd only known her a few days, I'd shared more of myself with her than I'd ever shared with anyone else. I'd been part of her aura—her spirit. This was something I knew would probably never happen again.

When I thought about dropping her off at her place and continuing my life without her, a feeling of unbearable loss dropped over me and an overwhelming sense of sadness filled my being. In a very short period, Izzy had become an essential part of my life, and I suspected that if I didn't continue holding on to her, I'd never be truly happy.

I'd have to break it off with Vera, of course. It was a blessing that she and I barely knew one another and hadn't had the time to share cherished memories. Considering this, I hoped she'd understand.

"Brad?" Izzy was watching me. "What happens now?"

"I don't think we can continue our lives as if nothing ever happened, can we?"

"We can't just ignore this. But we can't let it influence the rest of our lives, either. Danny's gone now, and I really feel that he's finally at peace. He was the biggest part of my life, and I'll never forget him. But I'm young and have the rest of my life to live. He wouldn't want me to forget him, but he wouldn't want me to stop living, either."

"I think we both need to resume our lives."

"Yes. I agree."

We both remained silent for the next mile or so. Then she turned to me again. "Do you want to resume your life with me?"

I could barely keep my eyes on the road. Had she meant that? Or was I reading something extra into it?

Just then, her hand rested on my thigh.

I swallowed a lump in my throat. "I take it you're serious?"

Her hand didn't move. "I'm very serious, Brad."

I was about to tell her that I was serious as well when she said, "Before you say anything, I'm sure you know by now that I'm very complicated."

"I already figured that one out. But it's not really a problem. I'm complicated, too."

"Sometimes my intuition gets in the way of things."

"No doubt."

"I need my alone time."

"My obsession with my company will probably be a blessing in disguise for you, then."

"I get bored easily."

I laughed. "I have a great jazz collection in vinyl and CDs. And also, a terrific DVD movie collection."

"I get tired easily."

"So do I."

Izzy watched me in silence, and I could tell that she'd gone into my head again. "Well?"

My heart was pounding, but it settled down the moment I told her what was in my heart. "Izzy, I don't want to spend another minute without you in my life."

She didn't reply, but her hand remained on my thigh.

"What about your girlfriend?" she asked after nearly a minute of silence. "Danny told me—"

"I'll tell Vera. She'll understand."

"Please talk to her, okay?"

"I will."

"How serious…are you two?"

"We only started seeing one another recently, so we really didn't have the time to get serious."

"I can't stand causing other people heartbreak."

"I know."

Izzy began staring straight ahead. "Too many guys just don't do the right thing when it comes to breaking up with a girl."

"I know, but I'm not one of them."

She smiled.

A few miles later, I thought I heard a beautiful trumpet ballad playing in my head. I was just about to mention it when Izzy said, "I think I just heard Danny playing his trumpet."

Without turning to look at her, I said, "Did it sound like *Trumpeter's Prayer*?"

"You heard it, too?"

"I think so."

She sighed. "It's Danny, then. He's telling us he's where he should be, and that he's okay and happy again."

I nodded, and when I turned to gaze at her, she was smiling through her tears. "Take me home, Brad," she whispered.

"My place or yours?"

"I really don't care…as long as you're there with me."

THE END

ALSO BY DAVID BERARDELLI

THE APPRENTICE
THE WAGON DRIVER
DEMONCHASER I
DEMONCHASER II
DEMONCHASER III
DEMONCHASER IV
DEMONCHASER V
STEPPING OUT OF MY GRAVE
ESCAPE CLAUSE
FATAL INNOCENCE
THE FUNNY DETECTIVE
JUST A SIMPLE ERRAND
COLORS
WORKING FOR A MOB BOSS
AND DARKNESS FELL
AFTER DARKNESS FELL
IN ANOTHER REALM
BEYOND RECOGNITION
LOOKING FOR A DEAD GUY
THE NIGHTMARE COLLECTOR
HIDDEN
AWAKENED
WINTER SCENE
THE PLANNING COMMITTEE